Sometimes, there is no greater pleasure…

She turned and cast the crystal chain to drape over her back, bringing the satin straps around her neck. I zipped up the barely-there dress, and it hugged the curvature of her ass perfectly. I attached the chain's clasp, and the crystal drop dangled elegantly down her back and swung gently as she moved. The wings of the angel tattoo spread to meet the edge of the fabric, loosely hanging around the small of her back. Jen turned to face me, and the dress dared to expose her breasts.

If nothing else, she has an amazing body.

At my reaction, she smiled. "That good?"

"You look absolutely stunning." I leaned in, wrapping my hand around her slender waist. "And now I want to devour you all the more, my little pet." She shivered excitedly, and I let my hand gravitate under the zipper to grab her ass. She wasn't wearing anything at all, and I ran my fingers between her ass cheeks daringly. "You're such a tease," I whispered.

Faintly, she cooed in my ear, "And you love it."

The Dominant

by

Aleksandra Amante

The Dominant

Contact Information: info@thewildrosepress.com

Cover Art by *Jennifer Greeff*

The Wild Rose Press, Inc.
PO Box 708
Adams Basin, NY 14410-0708

Visit us at www.thewildrosepress.com

Publishing History
First Scarlet Rose Edition, 2020
Trade Paperback ISBN 978-1-5092-3363-2
Digital ISBN 978-1-5092-3364-9

Published in the United States of America

Dedication

To the girl I once knew
who was scared to embrace herself.

Chapter One

She twirled a lock of her mahogany-brown hair around her index finger, holding my gaze. The corners of her mouth twisted up ever so slightly in a quirky grin as her sapphire eyes peered into my soul. She sat on the window ledge, one foot on the sill, the other casually dangling to the ground. She was wearing one of my white, button-down shirts, barely done up to cover her breasts. Jen loved to tease me.

I shook my head, smiling at her. I pushed the chopped peppers around in the omelet pan, hoping I wasn't so distracted by her gaze to have burned the eggs.

The soft shuffle of her feet got a little louder, and I felt her hips press against my bare ass. Her fingers danced across the top of my thong, tickling me. I pushed a red pepper overtop of the pan edge, and it hit the stove with a hiss. Turning the burner off, I let her hands brush up my stomach to fondle my nipple.

I let out a little sigh and turned around. She tossed her hair back, exposing her neck. I breathed in the light scent of her shampoo and leaned in, brushing my lips against her skin. Taking her earlobe between my teeth, I felt her nails run down my back.

"I have to go work, babe," I protested.

"Sure...sure," she mocked. She unbuttoned the single button over her breasts and let the shirt fall to the side, exposing her erect nipples. "Are you...?" I pushed her against the fridge before she could finish, holding her hands against the stainless steel.

She squirmed a little against the cold surface and let out a whimper. I forced my bare leg between her thighs and felt the wetness of her excitement. I kissed her right shoulder, tracing the outline of her tattoo with my tongue. My hand fell between her legs and played with her clit. Jen let out a little moan.

I let my fingers slip inside her and kissed her deeply, pressing my breasts against hers. I thrust my fingers deep inside, feeling the warmth of her increase. "Yes, babe, I have to work." I licked my moistened fingers and kissed her again. "Tonight. I promise."

She rolled her eyes, slightly exasperated. "You work from home. Isn't that one of the perks?"

"Having sex in the middle of the workday? I don't think that it's in the corporate handbook as an advisable work activity."

"Ha-ha," she replied sarcastically, buttoning up the single button again.

"Eggs are done. Eat. I have to jump on a call in fifteen and still need to shower." I plated the omelet and ground some fresh black pepper and placed a few chives overtop. "What are you up to today?" I asked, passing the plate to her.

Begrudgingly, Jen took the dish from my hand and plopped down on the kitchen stool. "Uh, I have an appointment later today. That bride, Christine, from Long Island." The fork scraped against the porcelain. "But I have to go by the dress store before to make sure they ordered the right veil." She looked disappointedly at her plate and muttered something.

We hadn't been together very long, but Jen was insistent on making a life of our own sooner rather than later. I was in no rush. Not only because I didn't care about officially tying the knot, but more because things with Jen were never a hundred percent smooth. There always seemed to be something that caused tension between us. There was *always* something.

When I had first met her, she was with her boyfriend of three years and wanted nothing more than to marry him. She grew tired of waiting and decided to see what being with a girl was like. When that seemed to work in her favor, she broke up with him, played with a variety of women, and then decided to try and court me. Jen and I had already become friends through consistent encounters at the gym and in the locker room. At first, she was intrigued about how I liked both men and women for such different reasons. It seemed innocent at the time, but that progressed into a very flirtatious attitude. Looking back, I guess I had thought it was charming. She was always bubbly and had a certain rebellious attitude I liked. But that rebellious attitude seemed to have some significant consequences.

"Babe?" I walked toward the bathroom and ignored her muttering. I didn't want to fight this morning. I changed the subject quickly. "Would you mind coming with me to a charity event tomorrow? I know you hate them, but I'd love to take you." I peered around the bathroom door, waiting for the inevitable blue-eyed stare.

She looked up with bright eyes. "Do I get to dress up?"

"Yep, it's black-tie formal."

A smile spread across her face. "Yes! Please! I

really want to wear that red dress you bought me."

"With those wicked black heels?" I called to her from the shower. I could imagine her bare back, the angel tattoo making a statement against the drop of the crystal halter tie. Her calf muscles would be enhanced by the height of the heel. I could feel myself getting hot for her all over again.

I saw her figure from behind the fogged glass door and my lips lifted. She stood at the bathroom sink, bent over, ass out, brushing her teeth, knowing full well I was watching. I rushed to finish rinsing out the conditioner in my hair and turned off the water. Drying myself off, I saw Jen peer into the mirror, applying mascara to her already full lashes.

She was on her tippy toes as I came up behind her. I took a handful of breast in each hand and squeezed them gently together. Wrapping my arm around her, I slipped my hand to her clit again and teased her. I whispered, "I want to throw you against the bed, eat you out until you beg to cum, and then fuck you from behind until you do." Our eyes met in the mirror and she breathed a little heavily through her mouth.

"Yes, Mistress," she replied, forcing my fingers deep inside of her. "I will do anything Mistress asks."

"What a good little pet you are." I let her lick my fingers and lightly slapped her ass as I left the bathroom.

Grabbing a black thong and a fresh, white shirtdress, I cast open the floor to ceiling drapery in the office and let in the day's light. Settling in front of my desktop, I brought up my emails and started my daily scan of task prioritizing. I put my ear buds in and logged into the call.

My thoughts drifted as I waited for my colleagues to join. Lately, Jen wanted to have sex all the time, which was great, but I always wondered if I should read between the lines. And she almost always wanted to take on the "pet" role rather than just be herself.

I really don't trust her, I guess. But she's never cheated with me...that I know of. She's cheated before with that Brian guy. So why would I think anything would be different with us? I know she's getting restless, but that's not a good reason for us to move onto another level.

In the window reflection, I saw Jen standing at the kitchen counter, staring at her phone, scrolling through the pages. Every once and a while she would giggle. She hadn't bothered clothing herself beyond a bra and lace panties. Despite my doubting thoughts, I smiled to myself—if nothing else, she was amusing.

Why not indulge a little more as Mistress and push my worries to the side? But...I am pushing them to the side.

I looked more purposefully at my screen, trying to pay attention to the CFO's financial review of our latest clothing launch, waiting for my cue.

I was muscling through my portion of the financing strategy for our expansion into Europe when I felt a light tickle on my thigh. I swatted the air, trying to stay on task. I finished the section on expected financial return and put myself on mute. Feeling another tickle, I turned to her.

"Well, aren't we feisty today?" I cooed at her. She had put on black high heels and stood, feet firmly planted, hands on either side of her hips, holding a feathered whip, taunting me.

I laughed, "Ah, fuck it."

I closed the drapes again, leaving my headphones in, and swung her around to plant two hands on the desk. I pulled her panties down with a fell swoop, pushing her down onto her forearms, accentuating her bend, and spread her legs farther apart. I was in no mood for extra foreplay and went on my knees to eat her out, stretching out her lips with my fingers. Licking lightly, I watched her eyes close in enjoyment. I took her in my mouth more forcefully and she gripped the table. I sucked on her clit until her knuckles were white and she bit her lip.

Mouth still occupied, I heard my name come up on the call and took a quick scan at the screen judging what the topic was now. Projected budgetary costs versus actual for our Milan fashion show next week. I unmuted myself and motioned for Jen to be quiet. She looked at me spiritedly. I had to sit back into my chair and retake control of the screen to go over the budget details. This prompted Jen to come between my legs. On her knees she spread my legs open. Her heels danced playfully behind her. Her breasts jiggled gently in the cups of her bra. I wanted to have them in my hands, in my mouth, anywhere...

Fuck, Jen, seriously, I need to focus...I want to throw you against the bed, tie those mischievous hands up, and tease you till you beg.

I felt her lips along my inner thighs. She slowly, almost painfully slow, made her way up to my thong and nibbled my clit through the fabric. My focus drifted between her and the event budget—

Goddammit, harder...keep your voice steady.

I looked down at her and she gazed up at me, azure

eyes radiant. She forced my legs wider and grabbed hold of my ass, encouraging me to slide down my chair a little farther. I was reluctant to comply, shaking my head at her in disbelief and yet still yammering on about how much the models cost per head and validating my choices of girls.

I don't like that, Jen; you know I don't.

Putting myself on mute again, I laughed. "You're in trouble tonight, babe."

"I sure as hell hope so." Jen came up and met my lips with hers.

I let her straddle me as I ran my hands over her back and settled on either side of her waist. I kissed the tops of her breasts in longing.

She looked at me with curious eyes. "Why don't you ever let me go down on you?"

I sighed at the familiarity of the question. "I've told you. It makes me uncomfortable."

Very uncomfortable.

She rolled her eyes.

"You're going to be late." I motioned to the time on my monitor. She shrugged and dismounted abruptly.

"Yea, yea, I know."

"You're usually——"

"Yes, I know," she snapped. I made eyes at her for her attitude and she stormed off to get dressed.

Finally wrapping up the call, I heard her fumbling through her purse in the front hall. I took my earbuds out and walked to the front door. I helped her on with her trench coat, and, moving her hair to the side, I kissed her from behind, wrapping my arms around her. "I just care about your wellbeing and career reputation."

"I know. I just hate planning this wedding. She's just been so difficult to deal with." She paused, seemingly having to think about the excuse. "And he doesn't make my life any easier."

I kissed her ear gently. "I know but it'll be over in a couple weeks."

"I'll be working late tonight with her. She wants to go over a rehearsal for the rehearsal dinner on top of all the other crap we have to do today."

It was the third time in a week this bride apparently had such demanding requests, which seemed to have Jen working very late. *Very late.* This wasn't the first bride Jen had as a client that was demanding, but working overtime didn't usually happen so frequently within seven days.

Benefit of the doubt.

"No worries." I kissed her again. "I'll be here. Just text me what you want for dinner."

Jen had been working with this bride, Christine, for a few months. A rushed wedding, for a soon to be mom, who was marrying someone who also happened to be one of Jen's ex boyfriends. Christine, although certainly into other women, was marrying this big-shot financier from Wall Street for nothing more than the convenience of his money. Jen felt obligated to take on the wedding planning—something about a prior promise she had made to the couple upon hearing the news of their engagement. Evidently it caused her a lot of stress, *or perhaps a lot of pleasure*, and I chose to stay out of it as much as possible.

I kissed her on the tip of her nose, and she left the apartment with seemingly little enthusiasm. I waited for her to get into the elevator before shutting the door.

Chapter Two

Leaving the apartment to meet Caroline for lunch, I looked at myself in the mirror. The bags under my eyes were particularly prominent today. I didn't sleep much anymore—too much stress, I guessed. Luckily it was sunny enough to wear shades. Throwing them on, I spritzed one of my favorite Tom Ford perfumes on my wrists and dabbed a little on my neck.

The wind was cold against my face as I opened the door, and I wrapped my jacket around my waist a little tighter, burrowing my chin into my scarf. Toronto was unseasonably cold this October. I walked quickly across the street and down Yorkville Avenue, ducking into the restaurant. I loved living in the city. It was one of the many perks of the job, as I made enough to afford it without worrying too much about the price tag of the area.

I scanned the busy, yet cozy restaurant and I saw her before she looked up from her phone. Caroline sat, one leg over the other, the slit of her dress tastefully exposing her mid-thigh. Her rose-blonde hair was strewn over her shoulders while her nails clicked on her phone's screen rapidly.

"Hey, Carol." I took off my glasses and set them on the table.

Putting down the phone to greet me she responded, "You look like shit." She rose from her seat slightly to greet me.

"Yea, didn't you hear? Looking like *merde* is the latest trend in Bella Vita." I half smiled and bent down to kiss her on both cheeks before joining her at the table.

Caroline looked at me with a touch of pity. "You guys have been fighting again? The whole marriage thing?"

"Well, no blow outs, but the tension is there. Jen's all about making roots and settling down these days," I said, motioning air quotations with my fingers. "And it's only gotten worse with Christine throwing it in her face every day."

"Hmm." She frowned at the menu. "Do you know what you want already?"

I was already stressed enough for a glass of red and wasn't that hungry, but I replied, "Usual grilled fish for me. Do you want a glass of vino?"

"Starting early? Yea, sure, why not." She cast aside the menu. "So, have you given it more thought?"

"It's Jen. She's a great girl but the relationship is a lot of effort. Too much drama all the time." I neatly positioned the menus on the side of the table and the waiter promptly came over.

Looking up at him, I ordered. "Usual for me please, and a half liter of the cabernet with two glasses."

Caroline, always a little curt, looked briefly at the waiter. "Kale chicken salad, extra cheese, no dressing, and hold the nuts."

"Thank you," I said to him on both of our behalves, handing him the menus. I turned back to her. "You never did like nuts."

She tried a smile, but a twang of concern dashed across her face. "You know she won't want to wait for another year, and who knows what that girl will do when she throws a real tantrum."

"Sure, but that's no reason to rush things. It's really only been a year and a half," I said, trying to recall when things with Jen really became serious. I shrugged. "Maybe it's just not the right fit long-term. I'm tired of the constant bickering, Carol. I almost think that Jen loves to cause trouble and goes out of her way to make it." My mind flashed to the image of Jen's flirtatious smile earlier when she had sat on the window ledge. "Don't get me wrong. I think part of her enthusiasm for drama…inspires her passion in the bedroom, but it's just so much all the time."

Caroline sipped her wine. "In fairness, you said you liked kinky, and you definitely got kinky with her." She shrugged a shoulder slightly.

"I know, but even for me, it's a lot."

There's just something about her I don't trust. Maybe I'm paranoid but something doesn't feel right.

Our eyes met. "Is she coming to Milan for the show?" Her tone was ever so slightly mocking.

"I offered, but no, Christine's wedding is the day before I come back, and Jen needs to actually work—for once." The wine was a familiar dry-sweet on my palate. "I am taking her to the charity gala tomorrow though. She seemed happy about that."

"And you? Not so much it seems," she stated flatly.

I don't think I care that much.

I shrugged. "How are things with…" I paused, trying to remember the name of Caroline's latest fling.

"Tiffany? Meh, all right, I guess. It'll be over

soon," Caroline said nonchalantly.

"Getting emotionally involved, is she? How dare she. She should know better," I teased.

Caroline looked at me with lost green eyes, shaking her head.

"One of these days," I continued, "you're going to find yourself in Jen's shoes and you'll actually want to settle down."

"Is that right? And what makes you say that?" Caroline's face was attempting to be stern, but she cracked a faint smile.

Caroline had ended a five-year relationship a couple of years ago with her then girlfriend, Sophie. Caroline was head over heels for this troubled girl and did absolutely everything in her power to make the relationship a happy one. Many, many futile attempts. Over the course of their relationship, Sophie had decided to take up some hobbies while working the club scene. In the name of generating sales, Sophie landed herself a drinking habit and became rather loose with her panties. It was a downward spiral and, despite Caroline's best efforts to shield her from herself, Sophie ended up in more beds than Caroline could ignore. It was an entire year before Caroline was forced to call it quits. She deemed Sophie a lost cause, the relationship labeled a disaster, and Caroline's heart became closed. According to Caroline, Sophie was the only girl she had ever fallen in love with.

"It'll work out in the long run, Carol. At worst, you're stuck with me as a lunch date." I winked at her. We had been best friends for years, and I loved her like a sister. Changing the subject, I asked, "When are you leaving for the airport? Do you want to share a cab?"

"For Milan?"

I looked at her with a dumb face. "I thought we were going to Ohio?"

Caroline laughed sarcastically. "Airport car is booked for eleven a.m. pick up on Sunday. I'll swing by your place at, say, eleven fifteen?"

I nodded. "Did you do the run through with Georgi? Did he like the changes you made?"

She sighed heavily and rolled her eyes. "Does he ever? Pleasing Georgi is like trying to force feed a teething two-year-old when all you have is lemon wedges." She shrugged. "I added some brighter tones and a bit of glitz. I'll send you the final looks this afternoon."

Despite Caroline's rather less than demure attitude, she was a wicked designer. She took all of her suppressed emotions and fabricated them into clothes. Granted there was a bit more black and gray tones than a spring line traditionally had, but Caroline always managed to make waves in the magazines. Georgi, our show director, and a very flamboyant designer himself, was always pushing Caroline to make changes that he saw fit.

I paid the bill and folded the receipts into my wallet. I kissed Caroline goodbye on each cheek, gave her a hug, and we split our separate ways. I had a couple minutes before I had to be on another call, so I ran over to the local florist. Picking out an arrangement of autumn flowers and white roses, I handed them to the shop keeper to ring up.

"Don't bother wrapping them up." The salesgirl nodded and replied with an undecipherable response under her breath. I picked out a little card and briskly walked, flowers in hand, back to my apartment. I examined the rose petals in the elevator light. White roses were Jen's favorite—hopefully this would cheer her up and help me survive another evening unscathed.

Chapter Three

The vase of flowers sat on the foyer table. The roses had already started to open further, and I fussed with them a little more. Jen was already twenty minutes late, and I knew she would take at least thirty minutes to get ready for the gala. She seemed distracted when she got home last night and barely acknowledged the flowers. We had ended up eating dinner an hour later than normal and after she said was too tired to do anything but shower, watch TV, and go to bed. I was too tired to pry more than one layer of the onion last night, so I had let pretty much everything go. I too was going to be glad when this wedding was over.

I heard the key slide into the barrel of the lock. A little disheveled, Jen pushed the door open, carrying an abundance of shopping bags. "So sorry. I know I'm late. I know we have to go." She was out of breath and her nose was a little red from the cold.

Almost knocking over the vase with the packages, I took the bags from her and placed them on the marble dining table. "It's okay, babe, don't worry about it." I tried to take any hint of annoyance out of my voice. "Go change and freshen up and I'll put these things away." I peered into the bags noticing some odd lingerie brands on the outside of the bags.

She called from the bedroom. "Oh, no, those are mainly Christine's. Don't worry. Just leave them there.

I'll deal with them later."

I peered in a little more. There were a couple pairs of Valentino boxes too. "You went shopping for her? I thought you were going to go get something for tonight." I walked into the bedroom closet. "For us, later." I hugged her from behind, moving her hair to one side and kissing the back of her neck.

She wriggled out of my arms. "I said *mainly* for Christine. There might be something in there for us too." She smiled wryly and removed the red dress from its garment bag. "Can you"—she motioned from the dress to me—"help me on with this?"

"I'd much rather take it off of you," I teased, taking the dress from her and unzipping the short, back zip.

Late nights and lingerie shopping? It was her job after all, right?

Jen stepped into the floor length dress carefully, balancing herself on my shoulder. The satin draped over her slender figure perfectly. The cool fabric provoked her nipples, which now stood on end. She turned and cast the crystal chain to drape over her back, bringing the satin straps around her neck. I zipped up the barely-there dress and it hugged the curvature of her ass perfectly. I attached the chain's clasp, and the crystal drop dangled elegantly down her back and swung gently as she moved. The wings of the angel tattoo spread to meet the edge of the fabric, loosely hanging around the small of her back. Jen turned to face me, and the dress dared to expose her breasts.

If nothing else, she has an amazing body.

At my reaction, she smiled. "That good?"

"You look absolutely stunning." I leaned in, wrapping my hand around her slender waist. "And now

I want to devour you all the more, my little pet." She shivered excitedly, and I let my hand gravitate under the zipper to grab her ass. She wasn't wearing anything at all, and I ran my fingers between her ass cheeks daringly. "You're such a tease," I whispered.

Faintly, she cooed in my ear, "And you love it."

I rolled my eyes. "Yea, yea. You're asking for it." I smiled softly, slapping her ass teasingly. "Go finish up. I'll call for the car." Jen disappeared into the bathroom and I heard her spraying her voluptuous locks into place. I stared out the window at the twinkle of the streetlights. My black dress trailed a little on the floor. I put on my glitter stilettos and shuffled through my clutch for my phone. I heard the click-clack of Jen's shoes against the marble floor. I texted the driver.

I projected my voice a little. "Jen? Pete will be here in five. Is that ok?"

"Yep! Yep! Almost done! Go down without me. I'll be right there."

I put on my long dress coat and repositioned a loose piece of hair back into my updo. It immediately popped back out. I let out a little groan of frustration and, deciding it was useless to spray in place, I headed downstairs.

Pete was standing outside the black sedan, waiting diligently. "Good evening, Ms. Jones." He was a tall and lanky man, always polite and of very few words.

I nodded in recognition. "Evening, Pete. Jen should be down in a second."

"Not a problem. Here, let me," he said as he opened the car door. "Pardon me for saying this, but you look lovely."

I smiled. "Wait until you see her." As if on cue, the

building door swung open and Jen walked toward the car. She clutched the fur collar of her knee-length jacket around her neck as a breeze gusted. The red satin gown became a second skin against her body.

Pete stood a little straighter as she approached and obediently motioned toward the open door. "Good evening, Miss Blanche." He took a second to collect himself before politely continuing, "You're looking lovely this evening as well."

I shook my head at him, eyebrow raised. Pete blushed red, embarrassed at being caught in the act of admiration. I slid across the back seat, making enough room for her to join me.

"Hey, thanks, Pete." Jen slid in beside me and proceeded to fuss with the strap of her black shoe. I zoned out as Jen started to ramble about the day. Apparently, Christine had a fight with her fiancé and needed some extra attention. Jen seemed a little too pleased to have been of help to Christine, but she was happy, so I didn't prod or question. A happy Jen was a happy evening.

As the car rounded the corner, the venue came into sight. The old train station had been dressed in event banners accented by soft colored lights that beamed up the sides of the station walls, adding a magical luminescence. Clear LED lights twinkled on the trees outside while accent mauve spotlights beamed from below.

Pete opened the door for me, and I came to the other side of the car, extending my hand for Jen as Pete patiently waited for her to exit as well. Graciously, she exited the car, and we walked to the main entrance, holding our dresses and one another's hands.

Presenting my name at the door, we received our table card. I heard my name being called from across the hall and looked up to see an ex-colleague waving at me.

"Go ahead." Jen motioned. "This is work for you and fun for me. Here, give me your coat, I'll check them."

Leaving my coat with her, I kissed her cheek as to not ruin her garnet red lipstick. "I'll find you." I walked briskly over to the man who had waved, my dress swooshing about my feet. I shook hands with the group of people. Everyone was either in the arts, in fashion, or trying to be discovered.

After what seemed like an eternity but had only been forty-five minutes, the conversation had become tedious, and I searched for Jen in the crowd. I could always spot her from a distance. Her hair, with its deep richness, was easy to spot. But this evening, it was the fire-alarm-red dress that caught my eye. I stared at her discretely from across the room. She was making small talk with another guest, doing her best to seem interested.

Could I really marry this girl? Or am I just trying to convince myself? Or am I so paranoid that I think I'm convincing myself?

I gave my head a shake to stop the internal conversation and excused myself from the circle. I scoped out the bar with the shortest line and went to order us beverages. "One glass of champagne and a glass of red, please."

The bar tender nodded to me and continued making small chat with another guest. The well-dressed man, beer in hand, motioned, a little drunkenly, for the bar tender to come closer. As the bar tender placed my order on the counter, he leaned in.

"Get a load of the ass on that girl," the man said, as he pointed with his glass in Jen's direction. "I talked to her earlier. She seems..." He winked to the bar tender. "You know, just that kind of girl." He took a sip from his beer. "And shit, I'd take her from behind in the coat closet any day—with or without a few of these." He started to laugh, and the bar tender cast me a glance of questioning.

I looked at the dapper man, equal parts annoyed, repulsed, and ever so slightly in agreeance and said, "Yea, so would I." Leaving a tip, I took my drink order and moved calmly over to Jen, feeling the man's eyes follow me.

"Hi, babe." I gently stroked her arm with the back of my hand and passed her the glass of champagne. I looked at the woman she was chatting with, attempting to be polite. "Would you mind if I stole my girlfriend away?"

As the woman nodded and excused herself, Jen turned to me. "How did you know I desperately needed this?" She planted a kiss firmly on my lips, giving me the slightest tip of tongue for a mere second. "Don't worry, I wore lip stain tonight. I can kiss you anywhere." She winked.

"I'm sure you will," I replied. I didn't turn around to see the man's reaction, but I smiled to myself, relatively satisfied how that had turned out. I rubbed her arm fondly, taking a second to run my eyes over the outline of her breasts. She shifted her weight, prompting me to ask, "Would you like to go find our table and take a seat?"

"Would I ever. These heels are killing me already."

"But they look phenomenally sexy on you." Placing my hand on her back, I led her to our table, and we settled in for a multi-course meal with people I only kind-of knew.

It was well over an hour, and the speeches had finally wrapped up. I was more than done with the people at the table and I knew Jen was definitely bored. We were onto the dessert course and I sipped my espresso whilst Jen fiddled with the cut strawberries on her plate.

"Want to bail?" I asked quietly. She eagerly looked at me and put her heels back on under the table. "I'll go grab our coats."

She nodded. "I can meet you by the door, but first I have to use the ladies' room."

I handed the attendant our coat check tags and texted Pete. He responded saying he was stuck behind the backlog of valeted cars and would be a couple minutes. Coats in hand, I decided to go to the bathroom too and collect Jen.

I could hear a man and woman arguing at the end of the hall. As I walked toward the bathroom, the voices grew louder, and I could make out the face of the well-dressed, crude man from before. My pace quickened as I saw a flash of red in the reflection of the floor.

"Stop it! Let me go," she screamed.

Running toward her, I shouted to Security over my shoulder for help. Entering the bathroom foyer, I struggled to pull the man off Jen. He had pinned her from behind, against the wall, his hands pressed on her bare back, daring to go father down. Jen's dress straps had relaxed significantly, and her dress was held up simply by the crystal chain. The back of her dress had been ripped at the zipper, where I could only assume, he had grabbed her before my arrival to the scene. Infuriated, and realizing my attempt at releasing his grip on her was in vain, I jammed my heel into the top of his foot, and he staggered away from her.

I took a stance between Jen and the man, anticipating another act of violence. The man collapsed and wriggled in pain and drunkenness on the floor. All hundred and twenty pounds of me seething in anger toward him, I waited to let my guard down until I heard the thudding of Security's boots fill the marble room. I turned and scanned my once proudly standing girlfriend, crouching on the floor, clasping her knees to her chest, sobbing. I draped her coat over her shoulders and held her head to my chest. I rocked her gently and waited until her sobs turned into whimpers and her whimpers turned into sniffles. Picking her up off the ground, one of the security guards helped me with her, walking us to the car. Pete was kind, offering me a sympathetic glance and maintaining his silence as he helped me into the car with her. We drove the ten blocks home silently.

Is it wrong to ask myself if she started this? She has a way of seducing without meaning to. The man was wrong to touch her but...oh shut up, now I sound like every jackass that blames a woman for being assaulted. Just focus on her.

Pulling up to the building, Pete helped me with her to the apartment door. Jen was silent still. Getting her inside, I undressed her slowly, watching her reactions as I did so. Jen's eyes were heavy, and she seemed distant. She didn't meet my gaze but stared in front of her feet blankly. I led her to the shower, hoping the water would help wash away the evening's events. I let the warm water run over her as I undressed to join her.

Using my hands, I rubbed the coconut soap over her shoulders, letting the suds run down her back and arms. Behind her, I massaged her shoulders deeply. She sighed a little in relief. I moved my palms to work the muscles of her back, letting the tension dissipate. I admired the detail of her tattoo. A tattoo I had looked at a million times before but always wanted to trace over and over.

I have a thing for a girl with tats.

I let my hips gently caress her ass cheek as Jen closed her eyes, letting the mascara run down her face. Turning her toward me, I brushed the wet hair from her face and took her in my arms. Her wet breasts were warm against mine. I felt her body relax a little more.

"I'm so sorry," I whispered. I pulled her in tighter and she gripped the small of my back harder. I felt her lips against my wet shoulder and my body shuddered in response. Her lips travelled up my neck, nibbling at my earlobe, her nails scaled down to my ass, and she gripped my ass cheek tightly.

Is this how I would be reacting if this had just happened to me? Probably not. Why is she so quick to bounce back?

Her lips continued to provoke me.

What had Jen and the man discussed before? Had she provoked the scene? She wouldn't put herself in danger just for the drama.

From the corner of my eye I looked at her, questioning her ease and recovery from the evening's events.

But she seems so normal.

Her lips met mine, taking my tongue in her mouth.

...who am I to argue with her advances?

I felt myself getting hot at her touch and all I wanted to do was reciprocate.

...cautiously.

Jen pulled me toward her aggressively. I reciprocated and pushed her gently against the glass shower wall, straddling her leg. Her hand, still on my ass, traveled between my cheeks, teasing entry. A look of mischief came over her face.

"Really?" I questioned in hesitant amusement. She nodded in a foxlike fashion. I took both her arms over her head and pinned them there with one hand. Leaning into her ear I softly asked, "Are you sure, my little pet?"

I hope this doesn't bite me in the ass later.

"Yes, Mistress," Jen replied obediently.

Time to get into character.

"What does pet want most?" I positioned my leg more firmly in between hers, letting the top of my thigh brush her clit.

"I want Mistress to have me. Fuck me." Jen's eyes met mine and I couldn't resist the innocent yet daring look she cast on me. "Please." She bit her lip, adding to her conviction.

I leaned in and kissed her soft lips. I could taste the sweetness of the champagne on her tongue as I took it in my mouth. Pressing more firmly against her suspended arms, I began kissing her neck, playing with her breasts as I did so. I licked down the nape of her neck and took her nipple in my mouth. I sucked firmly on it until she squirmed and pulled against my hand.

She moaned softly.

"My beautiful pet," I cooed. I ran my fingers up her inner thigh, pushing her legs farther apart. I let my index finger brush over her clit briefly. She was already wet with excitement. I let her arms fall to either side of her.

"You're not allowed to touch me. Is that understood, my pet?" She nodded in reply. The steam of the shower engulfed the bathroom, fogging the glass shower walls. My fingers danced over her clit, pressing a little more firmly each time. My other hand traveled behind her, forcing her to keep her hips forward. I teasingly kissed her neck as I pulled the lips of her pussy apart, letting my fingers slide against her wetness. I entered her and she let out a tiny sigh. Wrapping and turning my fingers, I played with her G-spot, feeling the warmth of her grow.

"Mistress," she whimpered, "I want more."

I smiled coyly, amused at her whining so early on. Champagne always made Jen needy.

This is the Jen I remember, before the push of marriage, before the mood swings. Just a playfully willing sexual partner. But now after champagne and drama?

"Fold your hands behind your ass, pet, and close your eyes." She did so promptly as I knelt before her. I licked her inner thighs and made my way up to her wanting lips. I took her clit in my mouth and started to feel her wetness drip as my fingers played with her. I slipped two in. Her breath began to get heavier and I sucked on her harder. I slipped another finger inside of her, adding to her desperation.

Jen fussed against herself as I teased her. She

opened her eyes and met mine. "Mistress asked you to keep your eyes closed, pet." She stared a second longer, daring me to discipline her.

Not tonight—spanking would be too much for her.

"Sit," I commanded, pointing to the shower bench.

She sat quickly. I forced her legs open wide and brought her ass forward. "Keep your eyes closed and hands off, otherwise Mistress won't be generous." She sat, quietly, eyes closed and leaning back on her hands for balance. The shower water was a comforting background noise and I could tell that Jen was in a secure mental space.

I took her again in my mouth, teasing her with my tongue until I could feel her pulsing. I slowly slid four fingers inside of her as she breathed deeply. She let out a moan.

"Can you take more?"

"Yes, Mistress."

I narrowed my hand and began gliding it inside of her. "Breathe." She inhaled deeply and upon exhale, I slid my hand farther inside of her. The warmth of her engulfed my fingers and I felt her muscles close around my wrist. Jen moaned, and her fingers curled in enjoyment. I leaned into her a little more as my tongue played with her clit. My hand fully inside of her, I felt her body increase in excitement. I watched her as she cast back her head and let her hair hang freely, eyes closed. Her breasts rose and fell steadily as I felt her squirt over my hand in satisfaction. I pressed my tongue firmer and her hands gripped the marble bench. I waited in anticipation, keeping my tongue steadily stroking.

Her breath quickened, and I felt her muscles contract. Her back arched beautifully, embracing the release of energy through her body. She sighed, letting out an exasperated "Please, Mistress…more." Her body quivered. I pressed my hand a little farther inside of her, rotating my wrist gently as I continued to suck, making her cum a little longer.

She let out a long sigh of liberation, letting her eyes open slowly to meet mine. I stood to straddle her legs, petting her wet hair and bringing her head between my breasts. She licked them as her hands held my hips.

Maybe it's the champagne. She seems too normal.

"You did very well." I tilted her head back and kissed her deeply, letting the water run over our bodies.

"I want Mistress to show me more. I want to do everything Mistress wants. I want to please. I want you to punish me when I disobey." Jen didn't cast her eyes down shyly like she normally did. "I want you to be a *real* Mistress." Her voice was overtly provocative.

I couldn't help but grin at her enthusiasm. "Patience, my pet."

Chapter Four

"You're sure about this?" I looked at Jen with concern. "After last night, I don't want to leave you if you don't feel okay."

Jen continued to flip through her phone. "Yea, I'm fine. I thought you could tell," she said playfully, looking up briefly. "Anyway…" She shrugged. "I have the wedding to worry about and you need to go to the show."

I zipped up my luggage and lifted the heavy beast to the floor. Jen did seem okay this morning, but she was a bit unpredictable when it came to her emotional state.

I looked at her as I fastened the zipper lock. "You can still come if you have a change of heart. I can book you on the flight for tomorrow and then you can just come back a few days before the wedding."

"Nah, it's okay. I have too much to do and Christine is a *very* demanding bride." Jen placed a little too much emphasis on the word as she walked to the window and peered down below. "Besides, the car is here. Really, I'm good. I have lots to do."

Or someone to do.

I silently sighed and grabbed my purse off the marble table. Like clockwork, Caroline rang the buzzer and I wheeled my bags to the door.

"Okay, babe. I will see you in a week. Please call

me if you need anything. You have Pete's number if you need him to take you anywhere." I leaned in and kissed her. "Try and stay out of trouble." I winked.

"Yea, yea." She rolled her eyes. "I'll try." With that, she blew a kiss to me as the elevator door closed.

Caroline, dressed in all black and pops of leopard print, greeted me with a kiss on either cheek. "We match."

Handing the driver my bags, I waited for Caroline to get back in the car.

"Well, only you can do leopard, but everyone can do black." I smiled at her. "Did you bring your extra laptop charger? I couldn't find mine for the life of me this morning."

Caroline nodded. "Of course, but you don't usually lose things."

"Well I never used to lend them out either," I said, sliding into the car beside her.

Caroline snickered under her breath, "Well Jen should learn to return things. But I guess at her age and with you always looking after things..." She let the sentence trail away.

"She's not that much younger, only two years," I protested. "Plus isn't it the person that counts more?" Caroline looked at me curiously as I continued, "Okay, sure, she's not the brightest either, but..."

"Jen's hot, she's dirty, and she's willing," Caroline said bluntly. "She likes being your toy and being babied by you. When you get to a mature state, like me, you know what to prioritize."

I laughed. "You prioritize returning chargers? Good to know. I suppose that's true about Jen, but if it's mutual, what's the harm?"

"'Cause she's also wanting more than you do."
I still don't know what she really wants.

"Commitment-wise? Don't you think it's because she wants the party, not necessarily the commitment?"

Caroline shrugged. "All I know is that you'll get annoyed by all of this soon. Either that or she will do something rash."

I looked out the window and watched as the trees sped by. The fall sunshine lit up their leaves, expressing and accentuating their deep colors. I knew Caroline was right, but I wasn't ready to act upon it yet. I had gone through enough relationships to know that either I had to pick one that fulfilled my sexual pleasures or fulfilled my relationship needs of love and friendship. Or, I could consider the third option, which would lead to consistent relationship floating and an unfulfilled need for connection. But one thing I did not tolerate for long was a pushy partner.

The next fourteen hours of travel went by surprisingly quickly. I worked while Caroline slept peacefully. As peacefully as one can having taken an abundance of sleeping pills and forcing herself into a medicated ball. Caroline hated flying, but I was used to her anxiety by now.

As the plane pulled up to the gate, I rocked her awake and half dragged her off the plane. I laughed at her droopy eyes. "We have to be at dinner in two hours, so let's go to the hotel, shower, change, and go for drinks?"

"If I see a bed, I will sleep," Caroline responded groggily.

I pulled our suitcases off the belt and we headed to grab a cab outside. Having only been to Milan once before, the city held a lot of wonders for me. But the one thing that stood out distinctly in my memory was the women—they were stunning. Everyone said Italy had fantastic wine and food. I much preferred my own version of dining while having a few glasses of robust vino.

Honestly, I couldn't help it. My eyes followed a fair blonde as she walked through the airport in designer skater shoes, tight blue jeans, fitted with a bust accentuating T-shirt.

I would love to see her between my legs.

I felt a pain on my upper arm and looked at Caroline as if awaking from a daze.

"Come on, stop staring at the ladies. Let's go or I'll pinch you again. You're forcing me to go to dinner, remember?"

I rubbed my arm and smirked at her. "Yea, yea, I'm coming."

"Not yet, you're not." She winked.

I rolled my eyes at her, and we wheeled our way to the taxi line up and hopped in a car. We checked into the hotel and decided to meet within the hour.

The hotel walls, in traditional old Western European fashion, were dressed in layers of rather ostentatious crown molding and intricate plaster accents. The room was almost a perfect circle with a bathroom adjacent to the den. The bed faced beautiful floor to ceiling windows overlooking the busy streets below. White sheers blew in the breeze, sending in the warmth of the day. The scent of basil filled the air from the restaurants below. I heard the clank of cutlery and dishes and the occasional car horn. I peeked my head out the window to see each street corner layered with chairs and outdoor tables filled with people having afternoon drinks. I breathed in deeply.

I would absolutely love to live here. The women alone would win me over.

Checking the time, I showered quickly and threw on a burgundy, floral dress and a leather jacket. Pairing it with some black flats, I grabbed my purse and went to go meet Caroline in the lobby.

Caroline stood, hair in a messy bun, wearing a different black ensemble and some spikey blue heels. She put her phone into her purse as I approached her. Her face looked a little glum.

"I just got a call from—" She paused, taking my arm as we walked outside. "From Georgi. He wants me to change my accessories again."

I sighed, a little frustrated for her. "What's the problem now?"

Caroline fished for something through her purse and pulled out her vape. "It's a new cherry flavor. Want some?" I shook my head. "He wants more *drama*." She motioned in the air with her hands in exasperation.

This was the norm, but I tried to further express my empathy. "He does realize that you're the designer, doesn't he?"

We stood outside the hotel as she puffed. "Oh sure, sure that matters when it's my name in the magazine but not when it comes to his show design."

"He's always been like this, babe. You always manage to impress the crowd and the press. He'll calm down." I scanned the busy roads, watching for a taxi to approach. "Taxi?"

She nodded. "Eventually, sure, but I don't see why I have to change my girls. He even wants me to rethink their hair looks."

Recalling her overly exaggerated doomsday-doll inspired hair from the rehearsal shots, I wasn't surprised, but I shook my head in supportive disbelief. "Add a glitter bow on a couple of them or a flower and you'll appease him," I joked.

Caroline let a stream of vape smoke escape her mouth and vanish into the warm night air. I breathed in a little as the wind blew my way. I could smell the cherry accent. "The way he goes about it is all wrong. I had to hear it from Kathy."

"Kathy?" I asked as I opened the door to the taxi.

"Yea, that new stage girl, that Georgi is obviously not banging but his boss sure is. I caught them the other day in his office." Caroline tucked the vape into her purse and we hopped into the white car. "He seemed very pleased with himself while she was on her knees." She gagged in disgust.

I flared my nostrils. "Typical, though, isn't it? New girls often feel that they have to bend to the whims of those above them." Recalling all the attention and various male pressures I received at my prior banking job, I shivered a little. "Happens to all of us at some point, I guess. I just wish women stood up for themselves more often and men didn't think they had that power. Maybe we just give it to them, though, too…" I let my voice trail off.

"Ah yea, didn't you get harassed by some guy at the firm a couple times?" Caroline referred to my previous boss at the bank who had decided to make passes at me in the office supply closet. He had pushed me against the copier, putting his hand up my skirt, asking me how much it would be to have a couple copies of my ass.

"If you recall, that didn't end well for him. I hit him in the nuts with a stapler. And then the second time that happened, he forgot his skype video call was still on as he tried forcing himself on me. I only got to slap him that time but the fact that his boss saw was just fantastic. She really finished the job by firing him and then pleading me not to sue."

She snickered. "You've always been feisty. Besides isn't it a bit of a double standard how that ended up?" She looked at me mischievously. "Didn't you do her after?"

I laughed. "His boss? I wish! She was a fox, but straight as an arrow. That being said…" I paused to pay the driver. We walked arm in arm to the restaurant as I continued, "I might have tried my luck when I saw her at a coffee shop a couple months later." I raised my eyebrows playfully.

"Was she as straight as she led you to believe," Caroline asked, obviously amused.

I grinned widely. "I think she thought twice about her husband after that."

"And people think you're such an angel," she responded sarcastically.

Lights glowed a warm yellow as we entered the restaurant. The smell of basil, warmed cheese, and fried goodies filled the air as the warmth of the room wrapped around us. I could see Georgi's bald spot from across the restaurant and I motioned to Caroline. The restaurant was boisterous, filled with people just arrived from their day. The wine was flowing, and first courses were already on the table as we neared.

"Ah, my girls! Come! Sit! Have a drink! *Manga!*"

Georgi was as stereotypical as perhaps any Italian man in fashion—short, gay, balding, and flamboyant with a side of *extra*. "You remember Francesco, from the house of Valentino, and of course Stephano, his assistant. This is Maria, from Cavalli, and her assistant, Tima."

"*Ciao, ciao*." I nodded and shook hands, giving cheek kisses to each as we were introduced around the table of fifteen. Caroline sat beside me, hand waiting for her glass to be filled. Putting my arm on the back of her chair, I reached across to pour her a glass and myself one as well.

"Carol, my darling!"

I looked up and took a deep breath, forcing a smile, as Caroline rose from her chair. It was Sophie.

"I figured I would see you here tonight! Georgi told me you have a fantastic line-up in store for us." Sophie took a seat directly across from me, letting the slit in her pink, sheer dress, expose her entire thigh up to her hip.

Caroline, visibly distraught to me, tried keeping herself together. "I didn't know you were helping to run the show."

Sophie filled her glass almost to the brim. "Oh yes, well, I happened to meet the director for the runway show in the spring for Valentino's fall line and I've since…you know…made some progress." She winked and removed her black shawl, exposing her perfectly man-made cleavage. "Enough progress to land me this gig. Really it's just ticket sales and the VIPs I have to worry about." Caroline nodded, seemingly collected, as Sophie continued. "I'll stay while it's fun, but I don't really have anything keeping me here." Sophie's voice seemed almost hopeful as she cast a look at Caroline, who was picking apart her bread, pretending now to be disinterested.

"Money is decent, and I get to meet all the designers. Sometimes I get free things." She shrugged. "And definitely some things and *people* are better than others," she stressed with a wink.

I looked at Caroline from the corner of my eye, watching her discomfort grow. I placed a couple fingers on her shoulder for comfort and she placed a hand on my leg under the table in gratitude. The both of us were exceptionally thankful when the second round of food arrived, and Sophie seemed to be consumed by her food and having drank enough to think she could make a quick move with Stephano in exchange for a free fashion house tour and possibly more.

"I'm going to use the ladies' room," I said quietly to Caroline. "You going to be okay?" She nodded and shifted her weight to let me out.

Washing my hands in the sink, I heard the door open and Sophie appeared.

"I was hoping I'd run into you in here," she said as she came to stand beside me and play with her hair in the mirror. "What's with you two?"

Oh, don't start, Sophie.

I dried my hands, barely paying attention to the question but not rude enough to leave. "What do you mean?" I watched, amused, as Sophie rearranged her breasts in her bra, enabling another inch of skin to be shown in the V of her dress neckline.

She checked out her ass in the mirror and sucked in her stomach a bit. "Ugh," she said, annoyed. I wasn't sure if it was annoyance with her stomach or with me, but she continued. "You know damn well what I mean," she snapped. "Are you two a thing yet, or no?" She flicked her hair back to apply another layer of bright pink lipstick.

Do you know you look like a working Barbie?

"Sophie," I said sternly, "Caroline and I are friends. Very good friends."

"Yea, yea, sure. Well you better fuck her before I try and get her back…or maybe I'll fuck the two of you instead." She put her lipstick back into her purse and shifted her breasts once more.

I rolled my eyes at her. "Oh Sophie, you're so full of shit."

She approached me, leaning into my shoulder, her firm breasts on either side of my arm, and whispered, "But really, I think I'd like you more."

"Lay off, Soph."

"*I-e*, it's Soph-*i-e*."

And I thought Jen was dramatic.

"Yea, sure." I waved my hand in the air in dismissal and left the bathroom abruptly.

I rejoined Caroline at the table, and she leaned into me and asked, "What happened?"

"She threw some stupidity around. Asked if we were together." I smiled comfortingly. "Don't worry about it." I placed my arm on her chair again and gave her a kiss on the head. "It's all good. You know I have your back."

Sophie rejoined the table but stole Georgi's spot at the other end while he was predisposed outside. She didn't even glance our way.

Caroline tapped my leg. "I want a light. Come with?"

I nodded, grabbed our things, and followed Caroline outside. We found Georgi, talking up his friend Francesco.

"Carol, come here! Come, come." Georgi waved us to join him.

Caroline accepted reluctantly and looked at me, willing me to join her. Caroline pulled out her vape and began by inhaling a deep puff. I smiled and leaned against the restaurant wall near them, enough to be a part of the conversation but removed enough to not intrude.

"I don't know why you smoke that thing. Have a real light. Here, take it, take it." Georgi shoved a pack at her. "Carol, tell Francesco your inspiration for the line." Georgi continued, seemingly unable to contain his excitement. "It's brilliant. I give her a hard time but honestly it's brilliant. It's as if Norman Rockwell meets Audrey Hepburn meets..." He took a puff. "Meets..." He took another puff. "Alessandro Michele." Francesco's eyebrows raise in interest. "Bloody brilliant I tell you. Just wait and see."

Caroline looked back at me, seemingly overwhelmed by the sudden flood of compliments. I went to stand beside her, giving her a small smile of reassurance.

"Actually, Georgi..." She glanced at me, almost worried to divulge. "It was my previous relationship that inspired me. All the trials and tribulations dashed with love and pain." She puffed deeply again. "It wasn't an easy line to design."

He rolled his eyes at her. "It was worth all the effort and apparently, the heartbreak. You did good," Georgi said with a slightly drunken smile.

"I look forward to seeing your show, Caroline." Francesco paused to puff and watch a couple of striking young men walk by. Rejoining the conversation, he spoke in a convincing tone. "I need a new designer on my team and, well, you obviously didn't blow Georgi to get here, so I'm expecting good things." He laughed. "Brilliant things!" Both men laughed at Francesco's exuberance and mocking.

Caroline let out a long stream of smoke, letting it blow above her head. "Well that's a tantalizing offer to even consider." She didn't let herself smile but I could tell that a seed of hope had been planted.

Shit, I forgot to text Jen. Damn it, she's going to be pissed.

I pulled out my phone, breaking away from the group a little.

—Hey babe, landed safe, just finishing up dinner. Hope you're good. XO—

Jen answered back immediately.

—Hey, yea, all good here. At Christine's doing last minute dinner stuff.—

—Hopefully nothing too bride-zilla like!—

—Nope, talk later, OK?—

—OK—

Surprised by the brevity of her text, I put my phone away, annoyed, and walked back to Caroline, catching the tail end of the conversation.

"Lovely to catch up and lovely to meet you. *Ciao*, Francesco. See you tomorrow, Georgi." Caroline air kissed them both and quickly snatched my arm, pulling me to the curb.

"Taxi?"

"O-M-G. Let's go, yes cab, yes. I need another

drink, but not here." Caroline grabbed onto my arm tighter. Laughing, I hailed a cab for us. Piling into the car, she sighed heavily. "Let's go back to the hotel. The bar looked good there."

"*Ciao, Excelsior Hotel Gallia, per favore*," I requested to the driver.

Leaning back onto the weathered, leather seats of the cab, Caroline looked at me with hopefulness. "Do you really think I could work for Francesco?"

"Honestly, babe, I think you could. But you know, I think you could do better." I corrected myself. "I know you could do better. You could run your own fashion house if you really wanted to."

Caroline waved the air in dismissal. "You say that, but you sound crazy."

"I'm not crazy. Look at how far you've come."

"Hmm-hmm. Sure, but it's all about timing and who you know."

"You got here. You can go as far as you want to."

The car pulled up to the hotel, I paid in cash, and the doorman opened the door courteously. Caroline took my arm again, and we walked through the foyer to grab a seat in the lounge.

Popping bar nuts into her mouth, Caroline looked at me and mouthed, "Sophie."

I shrugged. "If it makes you feel any better, she looked like a tramp."

"That's because she is one," Caroline said, chewing.

The server came over to us, and I already knew our order was going to be. "One double vodka-martini, dry, one olive, and a glass of the cabernet, please." The server nodded and went to fetch us drinks. "Carol, honestly, look at where she is in life. We're not getting any younger, she's no farther in her career, she hasn't learned how to establish her own path. And you know the biggest problem?"

"She fucks everyone and their brother...or sister." The waiter, catching her sentence, tried to maintain his composure as he put down our drinks.

"Exactly." I took a sip. "So, why would you even think twice about her?"

"History, I guess." Caroline played with the olive in her drink and took a double sip. "Seeing her just makes me so angry. So incredibly angry. I get that feeling of disappointment and...betrayal all over again."

"You were more than kind to her. You tried for months and months to help her."

"Almost a year." She nodded at me. "And sure I gave it a good try, but you know, I always think there's something else I could have done."

I leaned in and took her hand. "Carol, stop. You're an amazing person, and you deserve to be with someone who makes you happy, not someone you don't share the same values with. You know you can do better than Sophie. You might be playing the field right now, but I think it's because you haven't found someone who truly makes you laugh, makes you feel..."

"Loved. But you're one to talk."

I half shrugged, taking another sip. "Don't worry."

"About?"

"Remember, we made a pact, years ago, that if we're both cranky cat ladies by forty, we have one another. We can start a knitting club and read *Fifty*

Shades of Grey together."

"Ha! Well I'm a lot closer to forty than you are and plus, by then, I think you'll be teaching *Sixty Shades of Grey*," she cooed.

"Ha-ha, you're so funny." I rolled my eyes.

We both finished our glasses, and Caroline signaled to the waiter for another round.

Leaning into me from across the table, Caroline lowered her voice. "So, what did she really say you to you in the bathroom?"

"She asked if we were together and then made some rude and crude commentary."

"Don't save me from the commentary. Tell me," she prodded.

I sighed. "She said she wanted to take you back or to fuck you or maybe the both of us."

Caroline shook her head. "Fuck her."

"Rather not."

Caroline finally cracked a smile and let out a giggle, letting the issue go for the moment. "Cheers." She held up her glass. "It's been a long time coming but we finally got here."

"You got here," I corrected her. "I just run the numbers and put up pretty pictures. Congrats, you deserve it." Our glasses clinked, and Caroline took a long sip.

"I'm so worried about the show." She took another sip. "I don't think I tell you enough—thank you."

"For what?" I sat, amused at her tipsy gibberish.

"Thank you for being so patient with me and helping me with all the stupid color choices and the texture contrasting and the weird fabric runs I force you to go on. Not to mention all those late nights."

"You tend to pick black. I have it easy," I joked. "Plus, most of that was over wine, which always makes difficult choices easier!" I grinned at her, attempting to wink simultaneously.

"You suck at winking. Makes your whole face scrunch."

I laughed. "Thanks? I try for the weird-scrunched-face-wink look."

"You're nailing it." Caroline finished her last sip and put the glass down a little abruptly on the marble table, making it clink stridently. "Whoopsies."

"Come along, missy, time for bed. You have a long day tomorrow." I signed for the drinks to my room and held out my hand to help her up. She took it rather ungracefully.

We walked slowly to the elevator and as the doors closed Caroline held my hand a little harder.

"Honestly, thank you," she repeated but now looked me dead in the eye. "I couldn't have gotten to Milan without your support." I held her waist as the elevator climbed the floors. She leaned heavily on me.

"Don't mention it. That's what best friends do for one another."

The elevator doors opened, and I walked Caroline to her room, which was conveniently adjacent to mine.

"Babe, where's your key?"

Caroline opened her purse and started rummaging through it, whipping out a library card. "Here." She shoved it at me.

"No, that's not it. Who even has a library card anymore?"

"Forty-year-old cat ladies," she snickered.

Sighing, I opened the door to my room, offering for

her to enter. It wouldn't be the first time she crashed with me. She stumbled a little over her feet and threw her heels off at the doorway.

"You know," Caroline shouted from the bathroom, "you called me 'babe' twice tonight."

Removing my dress and hanging it in the closet, I tried to think back as to when I had.

"I'm…sorry? Don't I call you that normally?"

Appearing without her clothes and no bra, Caroline looked coyly at me. "No, *babe*, you don't. You call your girly-friends that but not me."

I tried my hardest not to stare at her suddenly naked body. "My sincerest apologies," I said somewhat sarcastically. I walked to the bathroom to brush my teeth. "I guess it just slipped?"

"That's a terrible excuse."

I rolled my eyes to myself in the mirror. I heard the TV go on and Caroline start flipping through the channels. I washed off my face and strolled back into the bedroom, removing my earrings. Caroline had already claimed a side of the bed and her eyes were almost closed. I crawled in beside her and plugged in my phone. Nothing more from Jen.

Ah well, even if she is mad, how is that any different than any other day?

Feeling tired too, I whispered, "Do you mind if I turn off the TV?"

"Nah," Caroline said softly.

My phone screen finally dimmed, and the room went dark. Caroline shifted closer to me. Her bare breasts rubbed against my back. She wrapped an arm around me, and I could feel the warmth of her breath on my neck.

"You can call me babe," Caroline whispered. "I don't mind." She paused and on a sleepy exhale, she whispered, "I think I may even like it."

I waited until her breaths turned into little snores before I responded quietly, "Night…babe."

Chapter Five

My phone alarm assaulted my ears, and I heard Caroline groan as she unwrapped her arm from around me.

"Turn that damn thing off," she said, slapping me in the face as she turned over.

I turned off the frantic buzzing and squinted at the bright screen. Still nothing from Jen. "Carol." I swatted her hand away. "I'm going to go shower but you have to get up too and find your key. You have to go fit models today, remember? We should probably have breakfast too." I got up, collecting her strewn clothes from the floor.

"Holy crap!" She sat fully erect in bed. "You're right, we're in Milan. I have a ton of shit to do." She searched for something to put on.

"Here." I held her dress and bra in the air for her. Amused at her panic, I slapped her ass as she grabbed them from me.

"Hey!" She gave me the stink eye, grabbing her purse and leaving to go next door only half dressed. "See you for breakfast?"

"Thirty minutes?"

"Yea! Okay!" The door slammed behind her.

I let the water run over my face, trying desperately to wake up. It was a futile attempt; I was going to look like death warmed over regardless of what I did.

Rinsing the remaining lather out of my hair, I heard my phone buzz on the counter. Peering through the glass, I could only make out a short message.

—Off to the rehearsal dinner. Talk soon.—

I dried off and took another look at her text. Then I typed one of my own.

—Ok, hope it goes well. I'll be busy today, helping with the fittings. Let me know how it goes. XO—

—Kay. Good luck.—

Feeling so overwhelmingly loved, I put the phone down in frustration and looked at myself in the mirror. Without Jen's presence, Jen didn't have much to her. I blow dried my hair and clipped it up into a messy bun. My eyes looked a bit sad staring back at me. I fluffed out my hair again, trying to add some life to my existence—it was no use either way.

Sighing, I went to throw on a pair of olive-green jeans, a black tank and blazer, with some black, yet girly combat boots. I grabbed my work bag and headed out the door.

"We don't have time to eat. Here, I grabbed you some coffee," Caroline said, shoving a to-go cup at me. "It's black, don't worry."

"Thanks." I struggled to hold the hot cup. "Why the sudden rush? I thought we didn't have to meet them till eight thirty?"

She looked up from her phone. "Yea, I know, but Georgi texted me that Francesco is going to be there to get a sneak peak, and I want to make sure that I have at least three looks ready. He called a few models early."

"Yea, of course, no problem."

"Car's outside, let's go."

Within fifteen minutes we pulled up to the studio

and walked up the four flights of stairs. Passing the models in the hallway, Caroline looked them over briefly, her brain mulling what she would put on what girl. She motioned for the girls to follow her. They trailed in after me as I joined Caroline in the open studio.

The studio was fairly barren, apart from the stacks of labeled storage bins and covered racks of clothing. Little pieces of thread were strewn about the oak floor, left from an untidy cleanup job. The bust of a fit manikin stood in the corner by the floor to ceiling windows. A long, old, wooden desk framed the back of the room, littered with fabrics and stacks of old magazine editions from Bella Vita and various fashion houses.

I set my bag down on the old table and looked at Caroline, already stressing about the task at hand.

She's so cute when she's flustered.

"Hey, Carol, do you want my help since none of the assistants are here yet?"

"Would you? Yes, that would be great. Can you find my rack and bring it out? I asked the girls to hang the garments when they got in. They should be steamed already." Caroline fished through a storage bin for a measuring tape. "Ladies, can you please come out in your basics. No shoes right now." She motioned for them to change.

I pushed through a couple racks looking for the right one. "You decided to call it *Black Magic in Spring,* right?"

"Yea, that's it," Caroline called, flipping through her notebook.

I wheeled it out to her, checking to see how well

steamed the garments were. "And you need the accessories?"

She nodded. "They're in a bin somewhere, same name."

I found the bin easily and opened it up for her. "Want me to unwrap?"

She nodded again, consumed in her work as she flipped through her pieces. Shoving a black-on-black floral piece to the fair blonde girl, Caroline motioned for her to put it on. "Can you please?" The fair girl took it diligently. Caroline handed a couple pieces to the other girls and they followed suit. The blonde girl, wearing the knee length, trumpet bottomed dress, struggled to make the dress zip. Trying to hide her annoyance, Caroline looked up from her book. "What's your bust size, dear?"

"Thirty-four," the blonde replied shyly.

Caroline's eyebrow raised. "Oh, I see." She took her measuring tape to double check. "Thirty-six. Just as I thought. This won't work on you. Swap it with her." Caroline glanced my way in dismay, and I shook my head in empathy.

Caroline was in her element, her mental wheels turning as she perfected each look. She cast a few comments to the girls, who stood in silence, but for the most part she hummed and hawed while she pinned and made minor adjustments. Checking the clock on the wall, she asked the girls to put on their shoes and walk the studio in catwalk stride.

Caroline glanced at me as I watched them. "What do you think? Good enough?"

"Even if I say it's perfect, which it is, you'll just say it's not," I teased. "It is some of your best work though, I'll give you that much."

"Again, please, ladies." Caroline studied the flow of the fabrics cascading over their slender figures. Her eyes suddenly darted to the door as the door below closed. "It'll have to do. Okay, ladies, can you go into the next room and wait for one of us to come fetch you? Thanks."

The girls left promptly, and moments later Georgi and Francesco appeared in the doorframe.

"*Ciao*, Carol," Georgi exclaimed. "*Ciao, bella, ciao*. So glad this worked out."

"*Ciao, ciao*." Francesco air kissed both our cheeks and went to stand at the end of the room by the window. "Please, bring out the girls, Caroline. I haven't much time."

Caroline looked at me, so I went to go retrieve the models next door. Ushering them in, I held the door open, enabling them to strut in without pause. Francesco stood, leaning against the window, staring at the models as they approached him, taking a second to pause at the end of the faux runway.

"Again," Francesco instructed. Obediently, the girls walked the simulated catwalk once more. "You know, Georgi—"

Caroline looked at him, hopeful as to his next words.

Georgi looked over to his buddy. "*Si*, Francesco?"

"You were right about one thing," he said, walking forward and shaking a finger. "It's as if the hardships and beauty of romance just threw-up everywhere."

Caroline looked at me with bewilderment.

Was that an insult or a compliment?

"Well Francesco, I told you…"

"No, you didn't tell me soon enough, Georgi!" Francesco turned to Caroline, shaking his head. "You are brilliant, brilliant my dear. Look at the accent on the dress lapel," he said excitedly, pointing to an exaggerated pink bow, accentuated by white crystal embellished peacock feathers. "That right there is the magic known only to those on a first date of blossoming love."

Caroline sighed in relief, clasping her hands. "Thank you. Thank you so much. Oh, I'm so glad you like it."

Francesco checked his onyx watch. "I must go, but I am very excited to see the rest of your work. *Grazie*, Caroline. *Grazie*, Georgi. *Ciao*." He waved fleetingly to me and walked to the door. "Georgi, walk me out," he instructed.

They exited hurriedly and Caroline trotted over to me quickly, wrapping her arms around me in exhilaration.

"Oh, thank God that went the way it did!"

"I told you it was perfect," I said, squeezing her tighter. "Congrats, babe." I gave her a kiss on the cheek. "You deserve it."

Caroline grinned widely. "My work isn't done yet, but it's a good start." She shook out her arms by her sides, trying to release the tension in her shoulders. "Okay! On to the next pieces. Ladies!"

The rest of the day I spent mainly working on my own tasks. The room was abuzz with activity and chatter in various languages. Occasionally, I helped Caroline and her assistants in orchestrating the looks on each of the girls, but primarily I just tried to stay out of Caroline's way and let her genius take over.

Chapter Six

My feet buried into the warm sand, the evening sun kissing the ocean goodnight. I took a deep breath, letting the salt air fill my lungs as the gentle roll of the waves lapped the shore. I heard the faint cry of a seabird as it flew through the pink sky.

Her arms wrapped around my bare waist as she started to kiss my ear. I closed my eyes as she worked her lips down to the nape of my neck. With her teeth, she undid the halter tie of my fuchsia bikini top and let it fall forward, exposing my breasts to the air. My nipples stood erect at the touch of the breeze. Her fingers played with them as she undid the bikini's back clasp. Her hands cupped my breasts firmly, massaging them together. I leaned closer against her. Her hand slipped below the band of my bikini bottom, teasing me. I squirmed a little and she hugged me a little tighter. Her fingers slipped inside my already moist pussy, making my clit hot and wanting.

"I want you," I whispered into the air.

"I know," she responded.

The wind blew hair across my face and I brushed it behind my ear, turning to face her. Her eyes met mine, smiling and gentle. Her hand grasped my ass tightly, the other caressed my cheek. She kissed me deeply.

"I love you," Caroline cooed, eyes glistening with the last of the sun's rays.

"I…"

****

"Wake up!" Caroline screamed through the door, pounding her fist. "We're going to be late!"

I sat bolt upright in bed. "What? What time is it?" I shrieked back at her.

"Eight forty-seven! We're already forty-seven minutes late!"

"Shit." I sprung out of bed, running to the shower. Evidently the afternoon cat nap had become a little drawn out. I had no time to contemplate my rather steamy dream about my best friend. I looked at myself in the bathroom mirror, my hair frizzy against my head. "Damn it, I look like hell."

I washed my hair as quickly as I could, shaving the bare minimum of my body. I threw on a pair of black leather pants, a fitted, gold sparkle tank, and a pair of aggressive, black, designer heels. Grabbing my tuxedo-styled, satin blazer and clutch, I dashed outside, letting the door shut behind me.

"Caroline are you ready?" I knocked furiously against the door.

The door opened, Caroline appearing in an uncharacteristically bright, fitted dress—blood red with black lace accents. Her black, strappy stilettos were very visible under the dress' above-knee length hemline.

Wow.

Slamming the door behind her, she took a second to glance at me, smiling coyly. "You usually reserve that facial expression for when Jen almost loses a tit in public."

"Ha-ha, very funny. Let's go," I said, casting the

way with my arm. I couldn't help but stare at her ass as she walked in front of me to the elevator.

"You slept through your alarm too?" she asked over her shoulder.

I struggled as I put on my jewelry in the elevator. "I have no idea." I shrugged. "We'll be fashionably late. Doesn't matter anyway." I eyed her up and down again. "You look amazing. Is that dress from a collection I don't know about?"

I should not be staring at her like this.

Caroline glanced briefly my way as she put on mascara with a compact. "Yea. I made it last week." She paused, fishing for eyeliner. "When I couldn't find anything I liked, and why would I wear anyone but myself?" She used the elevator door reflection to finish her right eye.

"I know you hate it when designers wear someone else."

"If a designer can't dress themselves, they aren't a very good designer," she offered.

I cast my eyes down her body again. "Helps when the designer is a size zero."

Caroline shoved her makeup into her purse. "Size four, thank you. I'm not a waif."

The driver was waiting for us as we exited the hotel. Sitting beside Caroline I could smell the light floral fragrance of her perfume.

"Tiffany is a waif, isn't she?"

"Who?" She looked at me, puzzled. "Oh, Tiffany." She waved a hand in dismissal. "Well yes she was...or is. I let her go a couple days ago."

"Over the phone?" I raised an eyebrow. "You seem positively devastated," I said dryly.

Caroline slapped my thigh. "Shut up. You know how I am. She was a nice girl, all hundred pounds of her, but once they say 'I miss you' on the phone, they have to go."

"I've told you that before, when you went on that three-month tour of Asia. That was a hell of a long time not to have my Louise."

"Yea, well, you're different. I actually like you, or did you forget?" Caroline laughed. "You really think you're Thelma? You're hardly the meek one." She barely lifted her eyes as she adjusted the crisscross of her shoe straps. "We've been friends for what? Nearly five years? I missed you too, idiot."

The car pulled up to the historical venue. The carpet was busy with various guests, dressed to the nines, and swarming with photographers. We got out of the car a few meters back from the carpet walkway. Caroline looped her arm through mine as our heels sunk into the carpet and she put on her smile—slightly bitchy, definitely not approachable, and yet somehow down to earth. Regardless of her bitch-face, the photographers loved her. I had intended to stay a few feet behind, but Caroline's grip only tightened, and I was forced to stand and smile with her.

"This is your night, not mine," I said to her through my gritted teeth.

Caroline wobbled a little as the carpet caught her shoe. Her nails dug into my arm, regaining her stability. "Shut up and be the person who keeps me upright in these damn shoes."

"Tabloids are going to say…"

"Would it be so bad?" Caroline turned her face to look into my eyes, smiling still, but cheeky now. "Suck it up. I'm half decent looking. Don't deny it, I know you were staring at my ass before."

I moved behind her, wrapping an arm around her waist, breathing in the scent of her lustrous hair as I switched to her other side. "I could never deny you or your ass," I muttered under my breath.

My comment earned me a playful smile and a little wink as we entered the building and made our way to the chaos of backstage. I could hear the clanking of hangers as racks were being shifted out of the way. Caroline trotted ahead, eager to do a final check on her girls. It smelled severely of hair spray mixed with the slight aroma of burnt hair extensions. I saw Georgi flailing the event program around in the air, beckoning at me to come over.

Georgi was dressed like Georgi in a bright purple, velour suit paired with royal blue shoes with gold accents, a white shirt, and an overly exaggerated gold pocket square. It took me a second to lower my eyebrow as he continued to motion for me to help. He pointed at a black-haired model with an unbuttoned corset. Painfully squeezing each button through the eyelets, out of the corner of my eye I saw Jen walking through the crowd. I took a double take at the girl, the tension building in my chest. She cast a look over her shoulder, suspecting eyes upon her. Seeing me judging, she let a small smile break over her face. It wasn't Jen. I sighed in relief.

Can you imagine? No thanks. I don't need that right now.

I did up the last of the, what seemed to be, three thousand buttons, and sought out Caroline in the crowd. We made eye contact and I motioned her good luck.

Avoiding any additional contact with Georgi, I left to find my seat in the reserved section of the floor. The crowd was already seated, and the first couple rows of the show were filled with A-listers and top designers, including Francesco. I sank into my seat before we locked eyes.

I sifted through my clutch for my phone. Amazing how a purse so small could still be a black hole. The screen showed one new notification from Caroline.

Recalling the look-alike, I scrolled through the latest exchanges with Jen. Barely any conversation since I had left. I decided to text her.

—Hey babe, show's about to start. I think you'd love it, the fashion for sure, if not just for the hundreds of shoes lying around!—

My fingers stopped. Then I texted again.

—Wish you were here.—

I knew the last part was a lie, but I sent it anyway. I let the screen go dark. I flicked it back open, remembering Caroline's message.

—Nervous...wine...vodka...champagne??!!! Anything!—

I texted back.

—Coming—

I searched through the crowd for the event server and paid her off with a bill for the two glasses of vodka soda she was about to serve another guest and headed backstage.

"Fucking took you long enough," Caroline said snatching the glass out of my hand. She downed it in three big gulps.

I shrugged a little and offered her the second glass. She placed the empty glass on a nearby table and held the second as if nothing had happened.

"Thanks." She sighed heavily. "Needed that. Sorry, didn't mean to snap at you." She buzzed her lips anxiously.

"Girls look great," I said, offering her some comfort.

"They have to look *fantastic*. I worked my ass off for this."

"You did work your ass off to get here, and you deserve to be here. And, FYI, Francesco is seated front row, near the end of the catwalk, stage left."

Caroline nodded, taking a sip of her drink. "Take notes on his reactions, will you? If he hates it, I need to be prepared."

I laughed. "Sure." I rubbed her arm. "It'll be great. Trust yourself a little more."

The lights dimmed, and the DJ started playing music above the volume of the crowd. People shuffled to take their seats and the camera flashes quietened.

I gave Caroline a quick nod, and she disappeared into the pit of models and sparkles. Taking my seat again, I found myself sitting next to Francesco.

"Hope you don't mind, *bella*," he leaned over and whisper-yelled to me.

I shook my head. "Not at all."

"Your friend, Caroline, she's quite talented?"

"I'd like to think so, yes." My eye queried toward his facial expression, which stared straight again and slightly pouted.

Lip filler? Maybe. I wouldn't put it past him.

He finished flipping through the program. "I don't make room for designers often, but Georgi seems so confident in her."

"She's worth the trouble," I said almost flirtatiously.

"For you maybe." His eyes flicked my way and a slight smile formed. He motioned to the stage. "We will see, *carissima*."

The room went dark for a second and immediately fell silent. The cameras stopped flashing. Francesco crossed his arms and leaned back against his chair, ready to be impressed. I let out a long, silent breath. My heart nervously raced for Caroline.

The music started, strobe lights danced around the room and then, timed perfectly with the beat, the catwalk lit up, strobes stopped, and the first girl appeared from behind the curtain. Caroline's first look was an aggressively feminine, predominantly black dress, exaggerated at the hip and underpinned with a blush-purple, satin layer. An airy train flew freely behind, lifted gracefully by the stage fans.

I scanned Francesco's face for something. His eyes pierced the girl as she walked by. I looked straight ahead again, my eyes a little wider, not knowing what to make of the statue beside me.

With the forty-five-minute show coming to a close, the last girl came out. The bones of her rigid, pink corset showing evidently through the black lace mesh layer elegantly pulled over the top. A heavily overstated tutu extended at the girl's waist. The tutu was multilayered in black, rose, and gold and dripped black crystals. The model's hair was braided and pinned elaborately on her head, exposing the large petaled rose affixed to her back. The rose's petals shimmered in the light as the model walked. The model's heels were edgy to offset the tutu stigma, and wrapped around her legs, to her upper thigh, in a thick black ribbon. The audience made a noticeable gasp at the showcasing of the final look.

Weeks before, upon seeing the first unveiling of the show closer, I had thought it was one of Caroline's best pieces. I looked at Francesco, and he kept his gaze unwavering.

Camera flashes lit the room. The models did a final walk as Caroline appeared from behind the curtain and she took a brief bow and made a small wave to the audience. The audience was clapping ecstatically, and now the majority stood. Francesco took no time to clap, leaving my side abruptly. He disappeared behind me, enabling me to take out my phone as I moved toward the aisle.

I immediately texted Caroline.

—Congrats! Francesco had poker face. Proud of you no matter what.—

I sent it quickly, almost tripping over the chair with the distraction. I headed backstage. I pushed through the crowd of girls and saw Georgi fussing over a girl. He motioned with the snap of his fingers over to the make-up tables.

I could barely see her, Francesco blocking most of my view, so I stood and waited. It was an eternity before Francesco left. Caroline, leaning against the make-up table, stared at the ground, emotionless.

"Hey." I took her in my arms.

She stood and hugged me tightly. "I didn't get the designer position on his team."

My heart sank for her. "I'm so sorry," I sputtered stupidly.

She leaned back to look at me and a grin spread

widely across her face. "Francesco offered me my own label under his house."

"A private label!" I almost screamed in excitement.

"Shh! Quiet! Yes! I don't want everyone to know." She couldn't resist the temptation to smile even wider. "Can you believe it!"

"Oh, I am so proud of you, babe!" I held her forearms, while we did mini hops in our heels like schoolgirls. I hugged her again. "You deserve this. It's everything you ever wanted."

"None of the paperwork is signed, but it's sounding good."

"The hell with the paperwork. We need to celebrate."

"Carol!" Georgi shouted, coaxing her toward him.

"Go." I motioned. "I'll wait for you outside."

She spryly walked over toward him as I turned and made my way through the buzz of the crowd. Select models were mingling with the guests, taking photos with A-listers as instructed. I searched for the exit, tired of the noise and the heat of the crowd.

The cool blast of fall air hit my face. Outside was almost as busy as in with people heading to the reception and the invite-only after party. I chose to lean against the wall of the building as I flipped through my email. It buzzed in my hand briefly.

—Hey, finally getting this wedding done. Thank God. Hope the show goes well. Steal some shoes for me. XX—

—I'll do my best!—

It was an uncreative response.

I think I'm over this. I don't think I care that much anymore.

I stood patiently outside, people watching as guests flooded outside.

"Hey." Caroline came to lean beside me. "That was nuts. It hasn't sunk in."

"It won't until you have a proper celebratory drink and wake up tomorrow to sign a contract. Come on, we have a party to get to." I tugged at her, leading her down the stairs.

The car ride was short, and we soon arrived at the Stella Hotel where an abundance of photographers lined the stairs. We walked arm and arm inside and headed to the reserved seating area. We had no need to flash our invites or passes. Caroline was well recognized by now.

There was a free flow of alcohol with bottles of champagne at every table. The server came by and offered us two flutes, but I shook my head and ordered Caroline a double vodka soda with cranberry and a glass of cabernet for myself. No point in getting a headache from the bubbly.

Everyone we knew passed by to say hello. It was a blur of hugging, cheek kissing, fake smiling, and small talk. Francesco waved from afar in acknowledgement. Georgi was nowhere to be seen but I could only guess he'd found a Milano muse to entertain himself.

Caroline leaned into me. "I'm exhausted. Can we go grab a drink somewhere else? There's just too many people."

I nodded. "Hotel?" I asked as we left out the back door. "Not too far to crawl then?"

Caroline smiled. "Not too far at all."

Avoiding the bustle of the Stella's entrance, I flagged a taxi and we headed back to the hotel. Caroline leaned her head heavily on my shoulder in the car.

As if star struck, she whispered, "This is everything I wanted."

I kissed the top of her head. "I know, you deserve it."

She sighed, buzzed on vodka and adrenalin but tired from the day. The taxi came to a halt and I helped Caroline out of the car. We sauntered slowly to the hotel bar and grabbed a low table, settling into the bench seating. We weren't alone but it was quiet enough to talk.

I ordered the usual and Caroline perked up in front of me. "Would you come?"

I raised an eyebrow. "What's that now?"

"I'm assuming I get my own team, but would you come be my financial director and marketing creative?" Caroline's face indicated that she was serious, but I knew she had a few.

"Babe, you know I would love to, but I'm sure Francesco will have his own team to provide you."

"Fuck that, you're the best at what you do. I need the best to be the best."

"You're the best already. You just got offered more than most designers get in a lifetime."

Caroline placed her hand on mine. "I'm serious. Would you come if I asked you? Would you leave your life in Toronto and come?"

I thought quietly for a moment, swirling the wine in my glass. "Yes, I could do that." And I meant it. I had nothing keeping me in Toronto, really. Jen had no hold on me, I had already moved from my West Coast family, and I loved working with Caroline. I loved my job and I was ready for adventure.

"More importantly," she continued, "do you want

to?"

"Babe, we've been down this road before. You know I support you, always, and if you want me to be there for you on this next adventure, then yes."

"You also get a promotion out of the deal." Caroline smirked.

"Well, yes, there's that too, but I would only go because you, and whomever, feel it's deserved not because I'm working the network."

Caroline nodded. "You know," she cooed, "you've called me 'babe' more on this trip than in the five years that I've known you."

"Is that right?" I couldn't help but smile. "Sincerest apologies," I said with sarcasm.

Caroline inched closer and placed her hand on my thigh, bringing her lips to my ear. "Is it wrong?"

I held my silence. My heart began to race.

"Is it wrong?" she asked again.

"You're my best friend," I muttered in a slightly unconvincing protest.

"Have you ever thought about it? About what we could be?"

My dream from earlier flashed in my mind. "Of course." I tried to maintain some levelheadedness. "But..."

"But," she asked back, "what could be better than two best friends?"

"You've had a few drinks, Babe, let's just call it a night."

She got a little frustrated. "Is it Jen? Because I can respect that. I just didn't think you were that into her."

"Caroline, I have always cared for you, wanted you in my life. You mean more to me than anyone."

She leaned in and kissed my cheek. "You're the only person I trust. And, you know what?"

"What's that?"

"You're really fucking hot." She laughed.

I shook my head at her, taking another sip. "As are you."

Before I had time to protest, Caroline took my hand and ran it up her inner thigh. Her bare legs were smooth and soft under my fingers. Our eyes locked daringly.

The silence of eye communication was enough to get the message across. I threw enough cash on the table to cover drinks and tip, too impatient to wait for the bill and charge the room.

Caroline took my hand and eagerly led me to the elevators. Doors opened, and she pulled me in. Almost forgetting to call the floor, I pressed her against the elevator wall, holding her hands still against the elevator rail. I held her there, my leg between hers, eyes closed as I took in the scent of her hair. The doors opened.

She kept pace with me as we traveled down the hall to my room.

The door shut firmly as I pressed her against it. Our lips hadn't touched yet, and I could feel my heart pounding under my gold tank top. I lingered there, my body pressed against hers, feeling her breath on my ear. Her hands gripped the small of my back, pulling my pelvis into her groin, teasing her clit on my thigh.

Taking her hand in mine, I led her to the bed, shedding my jacket on the chair as we passed by. I twirled her around to have her back toward me, and she let out a sweet giggle.

I melted at the sound of that playful laugh.

I moved her hair to one side and took her earlobe between my lips to suck on it. I started kissing softly behind her ear. In the moonlit room, I saw Caroline's eyes close as she embraced the moment.

Really? Was this really happening?

I worked my way down her neck to her collarbone. Slowly, I unzipped her dress, letting the straps fall off her shoulders. The dress dropped softly to the floor. She stood, red thong and strappy heels were all that remained. Her nipples were erect, and I ran my fingers over them, cupping a perfectly small breast in my hand. My other hand traced her abs and she squirmed against me.

Caroline turned in my arms to face me. "You have too many clothes on," she whispered flirtingly.

I raised an eyebrow. "Not my fault." I smiled. I kicked off my heels and we were almost the same height, even with her four-inch stilettos still on.

She began to unzip my leather pants and realized the leather battle ahead. "Off," she commanded.

Sitting on the edge of the bed, I struggled to pull them off quickly. My enthusiasm entertained her as she watched curiously. Throwing them on the chair, she came to stand between my legs, pulling the gold tank over my head. If nothing else, at least I had coordinated my underwear tonight with a shimmery white bra and matching lace thong.

I held her ass in my hands and she took my face between hers. We locked eyes and our gazes held.

Her expression changed to a much more serious tone. "You know I do, right?" she asked, eyes hopeful and fearful at the same time.

I stood to meet her gaze and nodded. I held her close. "I don't want to lose you. No matter what."

"You won't. I promise," she said, leaning down to kiss me softly on the forehead.

****

My eyes opened as the morning rays already lit up the room. I turned over to see Caroline's sleeping eyes, peaceful and content. Her mouth opened slightly, letting out soft breaths. After a long, lingering, affectionate hug, Caroline had pulled me into bed with her and tucked herself under my arm—heels and panties still on. She had passed out a few minutes later and I along with her.

I turned to see the clock. My phone alarm would be going off soon. I quietly crept out of bed and fished my phone out of my clutch. Ten new notifications.

Taking the phone to the bathroom, I started going through my messages. Lots of congratulatory words and a couple random drunk photos from Georgi, and then there was the text from Jen.

—*I knew it. You bitch. Fuck you.*—

I stared at Jen's message for a couple seconds and put the phone down on the bathroom counter as I washed my hands. I looked at myself in the mirror and a puzzled face stared back at me. I started to slowly brush my teeth contemplating what could have provoked that text.

I heard a knocking on the bathroom door, and I pulled it open.

Caroline stood, partially dressed. "Morning." She smiled contently. "Georgi texted me. Francesco wants to have breakfast."

All I could muster was a head nod, and an "okay,

good luck" mumble through the foam of the toothpaste. Caroline left quickly, dashing across the hall to her room. With no obligations for the day, I stood in the shower a little longer, letting the hot water run over my body. I closed my eyes, enjoying the cocoon of warmth. I could see Caroline's eyes staring back at mine, playful and kind. I wanted to hold her again and feel her skin against mine. Getting out of the shower, I checked my phone, almost expecting an encore text from Jen. Nothing. Leaving my hair to air dry, I put on my distressed blue jeans and a simple, dark gray T-shirt. Throwing on a blazer and a pair of Burberry sneakers, I grabbed the essentials and headed out for a walk.

I made a nearby local market my destination, buying a coffee along the way. I looked at it again.

—*I knew it. You bitch. Fuck you.*—

And then it dawned on me. I found a street vendor selling international newspapers. Yep. There it was, front and center of the Lifestyle section of the Sunday Times, a distinct photo of Caroline and me, my arm wrapped around her waist with a caption almost screaming off the page, "Caroline and her partner..."

At least the picture is flattering.

I bought two copies off the vendor and tucked them under my arm, taking out my phone again and sitting in the sun on a nearby bench. I wrote a text back to Jen.

—*Jen, I'm guessing you saw the Times article? You know the Press will write what they want. You know Caroline and I are close. I've never hid that from you. I'm sorry that you're upset. Let's talk about this when I get back. Conversations like this are always better in person.*—

Caroline's smiling face from last night flashed

across my mind. I could almost smell her, the memory was so well imprinted in my head. I closed my eyes and saw her peaceful face sleeping, her body only a few inches from mine.

Definitely not going to work with Jen. I can't live a lie like this one. It's not fair to anyone.

Even if we had never exchanged the words, or pressed our lips together, my heart belonged to Caroline. Perhaps it always had.

My phone rang. It was Caroline. "Where are you?" she asked.

"I was walking to…"

"Come back to the hotel, I need to talk to you."

"Okay, I'll be there in fifteen."

She hung up abruptly and I began to walk back briskly. My phone vibrated again.

—The hell with you and your fucking girlfriend.—

I sighed heavily. "Good talk," I muttered out loud. I approached the stairs of the hotel and found Caroline pacing the lobby nervously. She grabbed my arm and led me outside again. I leaned a shoulder on the side of the cool building stone as I watched Caroline fiddle with the papers in her hand.

"He wasn't bluffing."

I sipped my coffee calmly. "No, I'd imagine he wasn't."

"I'm not ready for this. I've done, what? Three seasons with Georgi. That's nothing." Caroline paced a little more vigorously now, her wedge heels scuffling along the cement.

"Hey, babe?"

Caroline stopped in her tracks. "Yea?"

I extended my hand, inviting her to come stand

with me. She took it. Her eyes stared intently into mine. "You're ready. You wowed him. You wowed the audience. You made the Sunday Times."

Puzzled, she looked at me. "Really?" I handed her a copy of the paper and nodded, taking another sip of coffee.

Caroline's face lit up as she saw the photo and then scrunched up again as she read the print below. "Jen must be thrilled."

"Oh yea, super thrilled." I rolled my eyes. "Read the review." I waited as Caroline waded through the text. She looked up at me with eyes ever so slightly teary. "Told you, they loved it. So, what's this document you've been flailing about?"

"The contract. Here." She thrust it at me, wiping her eyes with her sleeve. "Read it and tell me what you think." She fished for her vape and let out a long puff. "I was serious, you know."

"About?" I asked, skimming the pages.

"Wanting you as my commercial director." She waved her hand impatiently. "Go to section twenty."

I flipped to it and scanned the section. "So, you get full reign in regard to picking the team and have access to their staff if needed."

She nodded. "Would you seriously consider it?"

"Of course, but what about…" I looked up at her, provoking the completion of the sentence.

"Us?"

I nodded. "Yea. Where's your head at?"

"Career first, friendship second and…see what happens?"

"I can do that deal. If shit hits the fan, can you compartmentalize the issues?" I already knew the answer—of course she could. She was like me that way.

She laughed, sucking on her vape again. "Do heels push your ass out?"

I slapped her ass lightly. "All right, then…yes, I will take it into serious consideration."

She rolled up the Times, preparing to slap my ass again in return, but I was too quick for her and grabbed her hand, forcing it behind her back, holding it there as her breasts pushed against mine. She looked ever so slightly up at me. Our noses touched. Her lips parted slightly in anticipation. I could smell the cherry on her breath. I leaned down slowly, letting the softness of her lips join mine. I held her even tighter against my body, releasing her arms. I caressed the back of her neck, lifting her face toward mine. I kissed her deeper, wanting to exaggerate the moment even more. Her fingers embraced the small of my back, returning the affection. My heart raced in my chest, my palms grew clammy, and my clit began to burn with anticipation.

Chapter Seven

We touched down in Toronto in the early afternoon, and within thirty minutes the cab was pulling up to my building. I begrudgingly lugged my suitcases upstairs. I had texted Jen upon landing but there was no response. I didn't quite know what to expect but I took a deep breath as I unlocked the door. Simply no amount of breathing could have prepared me.

Jen was definitely preoccupied. She sat perched up on the kitchen counter, bare breasted, bare assed, and flaunting the new black designer heels I had bought her only a few weeks ago. Her hair was long against her back, falling to the counter as she rested on her forearms, pressing the face of a red head between her legs.

I stared for what seemed like an eternity, trying to register, trying to find words, trying to simply move. But Jen broke the moment. She looked me, perched on the marble. She had an air of righteousness about her and then she had the audacity to smirk. That smirk set the fire ablaze.

What the fuck do you think you're doing?

In the calmest yet sternest voice I could muster, I looked her dead in the eye and firmly ordered her to, "Get out."

The red head, caught seemingly by surprise, let out a little scream and clutched her breasts as she staggered backwards. Jen slid off the counter and walked slowly over. "Welcome home, *Mistress.*" Her words dripped with sarcasm.

My hand tightened on the handle of my suitcase. "Get the *fuck out* of my place."

"Oh gladly." Jen picked up her shirt dress from the floor, still smirking. "Christine, here." She threw a pair of jeans and blue sweater at the poor girl who struggled to put on her clothes quickly.

I kept the door open as Christine ran into the hallway clutching her shoes and jacket. Her sparkling engagement ring and wedding band were blinding even in the dim light. She looked so sad standing there waiting for the elevator, struggling to put on her single strap flats. I pitied her in that moment. Newly married, freshly used, and just kicked to the curb.

She looked at me, casting her eyes to the floor. "Sorry," she mouthed. I simply pursed my lips and shrugged; this wasn't her fault. The elevator doors opened, and the girl disappeared hurriedly. Jen, on the other hand, was in no rush to leave, taking the time to put in her earrings and fix her hair in the mirror.

"Jennifer, get out of my apartment." I stared at her in the reflection. "Now."

"Oh, look at you, using my full name. What happened to 'babe' or 'pet'?" She scraped her keys against the front hall armoire, leaving a deep scrape in the mahogany wood.

"Keys," I barked at her.

She removed them off her keychain and threw them at my chest. "Fuck you. Fuck Caroline. I waited till you were *ready.*" She exaggerated with air quotes. "And what did I get out of it? Nothing. You were a waste of my time."

With that she stepped over the door threshold and I slammed the door in her face before she had the chance to say anything more.

Locking the door and already wanting to scrub her from my life, I picked up the phone.

"Molly Maid Cleaning Services, Angela speaking. How can I help you?"

"Hi Angela, I need cleaning service for my condo downtown. When's your first availability?"

"I have two ladies available for three o'clock. Does that work for you or is that too short of notice?"

"Three is fine. Can I text you the address?"

"Yes, ma'am, to this number is just fine. Would you like the Express, Detail, or Thorough cleaning today?"

"Thorough. Also, do you also have boxes for sale?"

"Yes, ma'am, we do. How many?"

"Ten should be fine. Will the staff pack them if I provide the items?"

"We charge extra…"

"That's fine. I'll pay in cash. Thank you." I hung up and called to notify concierge of their arrival.

Walking to the closet I ran my hand over her clothes, all the things I had bought her, trying to make her happy. Maybe it was more my fault that I could never give her what she really wanted. I removed her section of hung up clothes, her sweaters, jeans, shoes, and all the purses she obsessed about. I laid everything on the bed, ready to be packed. Scanning the bathroom, living spaces, and kitchen, I pulled everything that remotely reminded me of her and put it on the dining table. Things can be replaced. Memories were harder to shake.

There was a knock at the door, and I let the two ladies in. I provided packing instructions to the younger one, and she looked at me with a little sadness in her eyes. I ignored it.

My phone buzzed on the table.

"Hey, Caroline, what's up?"

"Do you have my tablet charger?"

"I don't know. I haven't unpacked yet."

"You've been home for over two hours, and you haven't unpacked? What's wrong with you?" she asked me jokingly.

"Ah, yes, well…" I looked around the apartment, not wanting to stay. "Do you have time for drinks and maybe an early dinner? I don't even know what time it is, but I need to get out of the house for a couple hours."

"Uh, sure. I take it things didn't go over well when you got home?"

"Wine first, talk after. Let's do one of our usual places?"

"Wild Tale?"

"Works for me. See you in thirty."

I decided I had better change out of airplane wear, grabbing a fresh sweater and pair of jeans from the closet. I washed my face, pulled my hair into a ponytail, and left the ladies to scrub Jen out of my life. Notifying the concierge to not allow Jen back in the apartment and to get the keys back from the Molly Maid girls, I pulled my jacket around myself a little tighter as I exited the building.

I navigated my way through the meandering

pedestrians quickly. I heard the sound of an ambulance approaching. It screamed by barely hesitating at the intersection. I trotted across the street taking advantage of the break in traffic.

"Hey!" A man's voice shouted.

I looked around, seeing if I had somehow annoyed someone. A tall, partially haired, rather plump man was waving at me from across the street. He jogged over.

"I thought that was you," he said, a little out of breath.

"Tim?" I squinted a little, trying to smile and withhold judgement. "Hey, I didn't see you there."

"Anybody can pick you out from across the street!" He adjusted his scarf nervously. "It sure has been awhile."

I smiled, trying to ignore his more than obvious weight gain and significant hair loss. "Yea, about seven years now. Quite a while. Are you still over at Morgan Stanley?"

He nodded. "Took me a few years but I finally made partner a couple years ago."

"Congrats, that's huge."

"Large part in thanks to you, apparently." I raised my eyebrows, which prompted him to continue. "You remember John? Well John said you had talked me up in front of the board just before you left. I got fast tracked and made partner prematurely."

I smiled a little more genuinely now. "You deserved it. You always worked incredibly hard."

"No more than you." He shrugged. "Enough about me. You look amazing. You're in fashion now, right?"

"Yea, just got back from a show actually."

"You must be a model." He blushed at his own

pitiful attempt to flirt.

"You're sweet but no, I'm just the finance and marketing director." I checked my phone for the time. "It was great to see you, Tim, but I'm meeting a friend and I'm running late as it is."

"Yea, of course, no worries. Want to grab a drink soon?"

I nodded, knowing it was a false proposition. "My number is the same, text me." With that I walked off quickly, waving a hand as I turned.

Caroline was waiting by the restaurant bar when I arrived, and she gave me a quick kiss on each cheek. She handed me a very full glass of red.

"Sorry I'm a couple minutes late. I ran into an old friend from work. I think I mentioned him—the guy named Tim from the bank?"

"Tim as in the Tim you dated for a couple years?"

I nodded. "Just a year, but yes." I let my facial expression accentuate my commentary. "He put on a bit of stress weight and lost most of his hair."

Caroline made a scrunched face. "Sounds delightful." She paused, judging my rather blank face. "So, Jen?"

I rolled my eyes and motioned her to walk in front of me as the hostess escorted us to our table. I sat down on the bench seat and removed my coat.

I took a second to look at the wine list, familiar suspects by the glass and a favorite by the bottle. "Can we split a bottle?" I looked up from the menu at the blonde-haired beauty in front of me.

She looked wide-eyed at me. "That bad, hey? Yea, of course. I'm no stranger to a bottle." I ordered for us, not even glancing at the food menu. Caroline reached for my hand, trying to comfort me as I sat in silence. Her hands were soft and smooth against my cold skin.

Caroline asked me again, "So, what happened?"

"I walked in and..." I took another moment to reflect. "Jen was sitting on the kitchen counter, naked, with her client, Christine, between her legs and eating out her pussy like today's special." I swirled the glass. "That's not the worst part though, really. What's worse is that she had planned it that way, that I would walk in on her cheating on me just to hurt me more. She even had the audacity to smirk at me."

As the waitress topped up our glasses, Caroline stayed silent and stern faced. She continued as the girl walked away, "That's impressively awful. I'm so sorry." She looked a little confused as she too took a swig of wine. "Wait. Christine, as in that woman who just got married to some wealthy guy that was also Jen's ex? That's one sure way to fuck up two relationships at once."

I nodded and pushed up the sleeves of my sweater, suddenly a little hot.

"And you are..."

"Okay? I think? Angry...but I knew she was the jealous type."

She put down her glass abruptly. "Oh, do you think she did this because of the Times photo?"

"I'd venture a guess at yes." I shrugged. "Jen has always been a bit of a magnet for trouble though," I said as I recalled the incident at the gala. "And honestly, who knows if she just didn't want to screw things up for Christine and her ex. She's always been able to hold a grudge for years after someone has pissed her off. When she wants to stir the pot, she does. Before we left for Milan, I had to fend off some jerk at the charity event we went to. I always took her side, of course, but it wasn't the first time something like that has happened."

"She likes the attention," Caroline offered.

I could only shrug. "I suppose, but she doesn't know when to stop. Rather, she didn't know when to stop. She barely responded to my texts while we were away. She was working really late nights the weeks before, so I had suspected there was something going on, and she was just choosing to hide it." I let out a long sigh. "Anyway, the cleaning ladies are there now, removing Jen's evidence and cleaning the physical situation up for me."

Caroline laughed. "That sounds about right. You don't ever like to waste time, do you?"

"What would be the point in letting it linger? Plus, I would have had to break things off sooner rather than later regardless." I let a small smile creep across my lips.

"Well cheers to that. We haven't both been single at the same time, for a long time." Caroline raised her glass and her lips went from concerned to flirty. "It's about time too." Our glasses clinked. "I have some news, although not as juicy as that. Francesco sent his feedback on the contract revisions I had sent him, and he accepted the changes so far."

"That's amazing! That was so fast!" I beamed at her.

She motioned for me to calm down. "Nothing final yet. My lawyer friend is reviewing before I sign, but it's a good start."

The concierge still hadn't called to say my

apartment was done after we had finished the bottle, so we decided to stay for food too. Dinner was fairly upbeat with Caroline's news and, after almost polishing off another bottle of red, Caroline came to sit beside me. I wrapped my arm around her, playing with her golden-rose hair. I inhaled deeply, smelling the scent of her rosemary-mint shampoo. She looked at me out of the corner of her eye, finishing the last of her glass. She turned her head slightly, offering me her cheek. I took the invitation without hesitation, letting my lips linger.

"Let's." In my ear she whispered, "My place or yours?"

"Bed's still warm at mine," I answered, motioning to the waiter for the bill.

She snorted a little. "We're best friends. We are way past judgement here. Plus, we can walk to yours."

Who am I to refute that logic?

I paid quickly as Caroline excused herself for a smoke. Walking outside, she took my arm and we stumbled graciously back to my condo. We tried to maintain some sort of composure as we walked past the concierge. The man acknowledged us by name and called the elevator for us.

I could barely contain myself as we stood watching the floors tick, continuing to behave only because of the older gentleman present.

I wonder what this will be like.

I struggled with the key in the lock as Caroline felt me up from behind, her hands aggressively attacking my waist to remove my belt. Closing the door behind us, I pushed her against the door—the smell of cleaning solution lingered in the air. I pushed my body against hers, kissing her neck. My clit was pulsing in my jeans, longing to feel Caroline's tongue and fingers. I took her hands in mine, bringing them above her head.

"Fuck me," she whispered.

I can't be mean to you.

"I can't," I replied. "I will lovingly fuck you though." I pressed my hips into hers and proceeded to remove her jacket and top, leaving them to lie on the ground. She swiftly removed mine as she pushed me through the foyer and against the kitchen counter. "Come," I commanded.

"I'm sure I will," Caroline whispered with an obvious smile in her voice.

We entered the bedroom, the bed perfectly made. I gently threw her against it, letting the decorative pillows fall to the ground. I yanked off her booties and peeled off her jeans, letting her lie there in a bra and thong.

"Make this fair," she murmured.

I followed suit and undressed myself to underwear. Caroline scooted up the bed and opened her legs. She played with herself, rubbing her hands over the lace of her thong, enticing me to come closer. I accepted the invitation eagerly and came between her legs, pulling her thong down. I let my fingers play with her clit, sliding them down to see how wet she really was. I could feel her dripping and hot. I came to rest beside her, my leg over hers, my fingers still teasing her as I kissed her soft lips. She let out a moan of shamelessness and my fingers entered her in response. Her breasts fell out of her bra as she arched her back and I moved to straddle her. I kissed down her chest, removing her bra and taking a nipple in my mouth. I lowered myself to grind against her, listening to her gasp in response.

My body started to betray me, and I couldn't help but relinquish some of the control I was so used to keeping. My lips whispered, "I want you."

"Take me," she responded, "I'm yours."

I want you to be mine.

I moved down her body, licking her abs down to her clit. I played with her as she fought the urge to cum. I teased my fingers in and out, making her drip onto the sheets. I licked up her wetness eagerly. I penetrated her with another finger, three in total.

"More," she whispered.

I obeyed, sliding another inside of her. Four.

"More," she repeated.

I kissed her inner thighs to push her legs farther apart and narrowed my hand to enter her fully. I cast a look up at her. Her breasts lay perky, back slightly arched, eyes closed, hand rested behind her head. She was enjoying it and I enjoyed doing it to her. I slid my fingers into her farther, pushing a little harder as my knuckles entered her. I licked her clit with a desirable pressure. Caroline's hand came to rest on the back of my head and I eagerly obliged. I sucked on her clit until I could feel her pussy dripping down my wrist.

She gasped. I felt her muscles contract around my hand. I took her into my mouth a little more, rotating my hand gently.

Caroline let out a little cry of enjoyment, pushing herself into me. I waited, working my tongue and working my hand inside of her, and then it all came together. Caroline's back arched, she inhaled abruptly, grabbed the pillow above her head with one hand, and the other pushed me into her pussy harder. She let out a moan as I felt her squirt over my hand. I sucked a little more vigorously as her climax came to an end.

"Holy shit," she exclaimed, coming to rest her back on the bed. "How the fuck did you do that?" She was a little out of breath as I came to lie beside her.

"I listen," I replied simply. "Turn over." Caroline complied, sticking her ass out. She was beautiful, lying there, so exposed, inviting, wanting, and so trusting.

This is dangerous. I haven't wanted to please someone this much before.

I shifted her legs farther apart, taking an ass cheek in each hand. I spread her ass apart, kissing each side. She pushed toward me, tempting more. I bit her supple skin and proceeded to take her in my mouth. I licked her again, letting the slight saltiness coat my mouth. I moved up between her cheeks, rimming her. Caroline gripped the pillow to muffle a tiny scream. I smiled a little as I let my tongue continue to tease her. I bit her ass again, tapping my fingers against her clit. She gripped the pillow harder.

Caroline looked at me from the corner of her eye and let her body fall to the side. I gave way and lay beside her. She gripped the back of my head and kissed me deeply.

"I want to learn," she purred, looking at me dead in the eye. "I want to make you happy, but you don't let me do anything for you."

"You do make me happy," I replied, kissing her again. "And we haven't actually done *anything* before," I corrected her.

"You know what I mean."

I took a moment to think, moving her supple hair out of her face. "What do you think makes me happy?"

You probably know better than I do.

Caroline looked a little sad, searching for a response in the ceiling. "I don't really know. We've never done this."

I laughed at the redundancy of her comment. I pushed a finger to her lips. "You're my best friend, and no matter what, you've made me happy just by being there."

That, at least, is true.

"I know, and that will always be." Caroline forced a little smile. "I think I want to change the rules. Can I be more than a best friend?"

I let my hand slide along her chest, taking hold of her erect nipple. "Babe, can't you tell?" She looked at me eagerly. I gripped her breast in my hand briefly and came to rest my fingers around her throat. Caroline lifted her chin, luring my hand to clamp down harder. I smiled. "In time."

Chapter Eight

Since that night, Caroline had spent significantly more time at my place. I felt a twang of guilt that I had so little remorse for the way things ended with Jen, but I really enjoyed sharing a space, my space, with Caroline.

I loved watching her sketch conceptual designs in her notebook. The way her hair flowed around her face and how she would chew her lower lip. She became completely immersed in her work, letting her passions flow onto the page. Staying true to form, I was never allowed to see a work in progress. Throughout our friendship that was always the rule, but I always got to see a creation before anyone. Caroline was still exuberant from the Milan show, having received an overwhelming amount of positive feedback and support from her peers and her private clients. Her private label had shot up in sales and I could tell that she was feeling confident in her ability to create work that people desired.

With Pete away on holidays, I drove myself and was letting my convertible idle as I waited outside the design studio for Caroline. She had asked me to come with her to a fabric store out of the city and, naturally, I was happy to accompany her even though I hated fabric shopping. She trotted down the stairs and pushed the door open with a heave of the handle. Waving, she ran over, braving a gust of cold winter air. I pushed the car door open for her.

"Brrrrr. Winter is definitely here," she said, shutting the car door with a thud.

I nodded. "I already feel like getting out of town. There's fresh coffee in the mugs." I motioned to the two travel mugs and pulled the car into traffic. "Want to enter the address into the navigation?"

"You think of everything." Caroline fished through her purse for the address. "You know," she said as she dialed it in, "it's been almost six weeks since I sent my lawyer's revisions to Francesco." I glanced quickly at her as I made a right turn, trying to judge the expression of her face. "He got back to me today."

"And?"

She let out a sigh. "I'd have to give up my personal line."

"We knew this was a possibility, more likely than not."

"Sure, but there was still hope," she said as she fiddled with the handle of her purse.

"How are you feeling about it?"

Caroline sighed, looking out the window. "Honestly, I don't know. I can't imagine not having one-hundred percent creative control over some part of my work. Even if it doesn't pay as well, I do it because it's one-hundred percent me and I'm not pleasing anyone else but myself."

"What about the other option? Work for Francesco for a couple years, get the experience and the exposure, and then branch out. Your clients may return, or they may not, but chances are that you'll have many more opportunities to gain new customers."

She looked out the window pensively. "I also would have to move to Milan for the start of the fall launch. He wants to introduce me to the world as his latest *musa.*" She continued rather begrudgingly, "And he wants me to produce a wedding dress, one per collection."

"That all sounds good." I looked at her briefly, seeing the scowl on her face. "I know you're not a wedding dress…person…but you could make it a black wedding dress, and I'm sure someone would love it. You'll find a way to have fun with it."

She added a pout to her scowl and took a sip of coffee. "I guess," was all she offered. Caroline turned up the music and rested a hand on my leg. Except for my occasional outburst of frustration at a moronic driver, we stayed silent for the remainder of the trip. It was a familiar, comfortable quiet.

We pulled up to the fabric store, which was as big as a city block on its own. I raised my eyebrows as I parked the car, the doors looming in front of us. I had forgotten how big this place was.

Caroline laughed a little. "I hope you brought a book. I'm going to be awhile."

"This isn't my first rodeo," I said, pulling the corner of my tablet out of my bag.

Caroline almost skipped through the doors. Practically tossing her coat and bag to me, she pulled out her design portfolio and made a little nest in the store beside a cutting station. I found a chair and positioned myself within her things and watched as she ran her hands over the bolts of fabric. She would stop every few feet as her fingers felt something desirable. She was in her element. She lost focus, seeing the trims and hundreds of buttons on the wall, and scampered over like a child in a toy store. The staff knew not to bother her—she was a regular customer and probably bought enough to pay their rent.

I settled into my chair, opening my tablet. I worked on the budget for next year's in-store promo of the spring line. I started to wonder if this would be my last season with Georgi's team.

It would be nice to have a change.

Caroline came fluttering back. "Oh, I love this, just look at it." She shoved a bolt of iridescent black fabric in front of me.

I looked at it and back at her, trying to smile and appreciate what she saw.

She giggled again. "I need this." Her red-blonde hair fell around her exuberant face, framing her sparkling eyes.

She's so pretty when she's happy.

I couldn't help but smile. "You've got the budget for it, so why not?"

"You make my budget, and it's always generous." She shook her head, laughing. "This time especially— it's nowhere near what I was supposed to get."

"So, sue me, I'm a little biased, always have been." I gazed up at her. "Will you use it if you have it?" I asked, motioning toward the fabric.

"Of course! Oh, I'll just take a few yards. No one will even notice." Caroline proceeded to cut off more yards than I think she had even planned and folded it up to the side, tagging it herself. This continued for another two hours, and her stack of fabrics grew to a small mountain. Caroline was selecting the buttons and finishes now. The store clerk came to me and asked if she could start ringing it up. I nodded.

"What do you like better?" Caroline held out her palms with a selection of buttons. She played with a shiny black and gold one with her thumb. I pointed to it knowing that her hint was less than subtle, but subconsciously done.

"Oh good, that one was my favorite too," she said, taking a bag of them from her basket. "Okay, I think I'm done."

I looked at her and couldn't help but grin. "For now."

The store clerk came back and took the rest of Caroline's choices to the check-out counter. Two large storage boxes had been prepped with Caroline's fabrics, and the bill was already well north of four figures. Caroline handed the lady her corporate card as I started loading the boxes into my tiny sports car. Two boxes in and I had very little room for anything else. Caroline came out holding her two bags of buttons of trims.

"I can fit one, but you'll have to have the other between your legs." I motioned to my full trunk.

"Between my legs? Then where will you fit?"

"Ha-ha, very funny," I retorted, amused, and opened the car door for her.

Pulling out of the lot, I asked, "Do you want to go for dinner, or do you want me to make something?" Before she could answer my phone rang. It was Jen. I grunted, already annoyed.

There would never be a good time to handle this. Better now than later, I guess.

I pressed the call answer button on my steering wheel. "Hey, Jen, in the car, you're on speaker."

"Hey," her voice was soft.

"What's up?" My tone was noticeably aggravated already.

She took a second to respond. "Maybe this isn't a good time."

I let a tinge more of annoyance show in my voice. "It's fine. What do you need?"

"Well, I think you sent me something of yours by accident. It's that red cashmere sweater with pearl buttons."

I tried to think back, recalling the red sweater she had given me for my birthday earlier this year. I had included it in the pile of clothes for the Molly Maids to pack. "Don't worry about it, just keep it."

Her voice became even softer. "Oh, okay." Her voice cracked a little. "It's just that, well, I miss you."

"Jen, is there anything else you wanted to discuss beyond the sweater?"

"No, I just wanted to…"

"I hope you have a good night, Jen. If anything else comes up, please email me and I will look after it promptly." I hung up before she had time to respond.

Caroline looked at me. "You okay?"

I shrugged. "Sure, I'm fine. She was bound to call at some point for whatever reason." The call had annoyed me more than I should have let it. "Do you mind if we just go back to my place? I think I have something in the freezer. How does grilled chicken sound?" Caroline nodded and her hand resumed its position on my thigh, her thumb rubbing back and forth in empathy.

The drive going home was quick, and I let the building valet park the car. I disrobed, putting on a long T-shirt dress, giving Caroline one as well. I pulled the chicken breasts out of the freezer, pre-heated the oven, and searched through the fridge for some sort of side dish.

"Babe, you good with…carrots? Broccoli? Or maybe a tomato salad?"

I felt the warmth of her embrace as she peeked over my shoulder. "I don't really care. Whatever is easiest," she responded lightly.

I grabbed the pre-cut, pre-washed broccoli and threw it into a pan with some vegetable stock. Adding a bit of chopped onion, I pushed the broccoli around, trying to distract myself.

"Why?"

I rummaged through the spice drawer. "Why what?" I heard a metal clink on the counter. Looking up at the sound, I smirked a little. "Where'd you find that? I don't usually leave that lying around for wandering eyes."

"What is it?" She took the leather harness in her hands.

I took it from her, coming around the counter to hold her from behind. I placed the harness over her t-shirt and let it cup her breasts. Folding her arms back, I clipped her wrists into the restraints and fastened the shoulder stays. Her body rested into mine as I pulled the wrist restraints toward me.

I whispered in her ear from behind her, "It's for when I want to do naughty things to you, and you try to resist, or, better yet, when you disobey."

She tilted her head back to rest against my chest, her gaze cast upwards to meet mine. "Show me?"

I could smell the broccoli on the stovetop starting to burn. "Hold on." I went to shut off the burner. "I'm a little hesitant to show you," I admitted as I came back around and undid the harness' buckles, laying it on the counter again.

She looked at me curiously and seemingly a little disappointed. "Why's that?"

You have my heart and I don't want to admit it. And all of this scares me half to death.

I hugged her closely. "Because I know what we have, and I don't want to risk it by pushing your boundaries...our boundaries."

"I trust you."

"I know. I trust you too. It's just that what we have is so wonderful. It's the first time I've been able to really enjoy the person I'm with. I don't want to lose that."

And I'm starting to fall for you, and I don't know what to do. I don't know how to handle this.

She turned to face me, taking my face between her warm hands. "I have to confess." She took a deep breath. "I've always had my walls, my defenses, my ways of dealing with...clingy girls. With you, I've always been able to be myself. I don't worry, I don't wonder, I just am. I can't do that with anyone but you."

I propped her up onto the counter, coming between her legs. "That's exactly why I worry. It's the same way for me. You know I have trust issues, regardless of my recent relationship issues. My walls are always up. With you, they come down."

"But not all the way."

I don't know how to bring them down all the way.

I admitted, "No, not all the way, but things change." I leaned in, so our noses touched. "You can change that. You already have started to."

Her soft lips embraced mine, the linger of cherry forever present on her tongue. I slid my hand up the back of her shirt, pulling her tighter. Her hair fell, enveloping our faces. She wrapped her legs around my waist, pulling myself toward her. We stayed still for a few moments, letting ourselves enjoy the embrace.

Chapter Nine

"Hold on," Caroline snapped. "You're truly terrible at standing still."

I hated being the fit model more than I hated going to the fabric store. "Well, I should be working on your new budget but instead you have me playing as your dress-up doll," I protested.

Her green eyes looked up at me. "Yea, well, I needed a tall, size four for this fitting and since these new fit models are seemingly unreliable, you're the next best thing."

I stood on the apple box as Caroline pinned the flouncy hem of the otherwise slender skirt. She had made the outfit this morning after coming out of the shower, body still half wet but full of inspiration. Caroline had been a flurry of emotions since she signed with Francesco. He had requested ten samples for the launch, and she had been working almost around the clock.

She slapped my stomach. "Suck it in."

"Hey! I'm flat," I protested.

"Yea, well, be concave. Remember, you're pretending that you live off kale."

"Yes, Ma'am." I rolled my eyes, sucking in my stomach. She proceeded to pin up the skirt waist and take in the matching top another couple millimeters.

"Turn," she commanded. "So, what do you think?"

She looked sternly into the mirror, arms crossed.

I looked at my reflection and for once I felt genuinely pretty. "It's stunning," I replied. I was wearing a form fitting, navy suit—mermaid skirt bottom with an exceptionally tailored, sleeveless top with sweetheart neckline. The skirt hem was trimmed with a fine silver, intricate rope detail.

"Here," she said, passing me a silver belt and a pair of nude pumps. I complied, and she stepped back and took a look at her work. She nodded to herself. "Well, I can honestly say that I'd very much like to devour you in that."

I tittered. "I'd be happy to submit but I doubt this skirt will hold up to it, let alone the top. A girl has to breathe. This is very reasonable for your debut, especially for you."

Caroline shrugged. "Part of the deal. I have to make some pieces for the *Modern Working Milano*, five for him and five of my choice."

"Well..." I turned to face her, towering over her tiny frame. "It's a two-year contract. There's already an end in sight if you hate it. Plus, you'll get the experience of living in an entirely different part of the world." I turned her and rubbed her shoulders. "It'll be fun, you'll see."

"It's a lot of pressure..."

I stepped down from the box and took her hands in mine. "My lovely Carol, you will be fantastic. You have the creative talent and the drive. This opportunity didn't fall in your lap, you earned it."

"When are you coming to join me? What day again?" She fixed something on the edge of the top's sleeve, something only she could see that needed fixing.

I tried to stay still as I saw the pins go in. "I have to tie up some things for Georgi, but I'll be there at the start of the new year."

"That's a long time."

I'll miss you too. Trust me. More than I want to.

"It's a couple weeks." I smiled. "Look at you, getting all attached."

She rolled her eyes and pulled away from me. "Oh, shut up." She swatted the air dismissively. "Take that off and put this on."

I stripped down in front of her, careful not to dislodge a pin or stab myself. I took the black garment from her. This was definitely a Caroline pick.

She watched me undress before her, amused that I didn't bother with any modesty when it was just her and me, even if we were at the studio. Still watching me, she asked, "So, you'll be there for the first show?"

"Wouldn't miss it for the world." I pulled up the side seam zipper. "I know you're stressed out, but I promise it'll work out. If shit hits the fan we can run away together, buy a yacht, and sail to Monaco."

"More like steal a yacht and sail past Monaco to somewhere we don't have to sell a kidney to buy dinner," she muttered, holding pins between her lips as she kneeled fixing the dress' inner lining. "Don't turn to face the mirror. I need the light from the window."

I looked down at the black, gauzy material. "Isn't this that fabric we bought a few weeks ago?"

"Maybe?" She smiled up at me. "They won't notice. It's just so pretty. Call it part of my severance package?"

I laughed. "You resigned, remember?"

"I'm sure Georgi got a decent finder's fee of some

sort from Francesco."

I winked at her. "I'm sure he did, just maybe not in the traditional monetary form."

"I think *that form* is the traditional method," she joked.

"I better be careful then!"

For that she slapped my ass. "This cute ass is mine, no one else's."

"I don't think there's too many people who want this ass my dear, but for yours, all the girls will be lining up. When I come join you in a couple weeks, who knows what I'll walk in on." I had meant it in a completely joking manner, but as soon as the words came out of my mouth, I knew it sounded confrontational. I cringed a little, expecting a blowout, just as Jen would have reacted.

Caroline let my arm fall to my side and came to face me, very serious in nature. "I need you to promise me something."

I took a deep breath. "Of course, anything."

She took my hand in hers. "If I give you all of me, will you do the same?"

"You already have all of me," I said quietly, almost as if I was scared to admit it out loud.

I already love you more than you love me.

"You have given me everything you know how to, and I respect and appreciate that, but I also know you don't trust me entirely." I opened my mouth in protest, but she continued. "I know you were kidding, but the whole Jen thing didn't help your confidence in people, or for that matter, in me."

"I'm sorry, it's just...I don't know how to let down my walls more than I already have. With you, believe me when I say, I get to just be me."

Caroline nodded understandingly. "I'm aware. You know that I have similar issues, but you've helped me appreciate actually being with someone. I actually want to be here. I am dreading our upcoming couple weeks apart because I won't have my *Thelma*. So, why don't we make a deal? I promise I will do my best to be the person you can trust and hopefully learn to bring down all your walls. In exchange, I need you to keep my heart intact."

I wrapped my arms loosely around her. "I can do that deal." Recalling our chat in Milan not too long ago, I gently asked, "What happened to us just being friends?"

She took a second to shrug. "We're best friends, but I think we make a great couple too."

"True." I nodded.

Thank God. Being in love with your best friend would be bad if it wasn't reciprocated.

"One more thing. I want you to show me this whole, alternate sex universe you seem to be an active participant of." She made circle motions in the air.

"You might despise it." I cocked my head at her. "And it's not like a club for weird sex people. It's just a different flavor."

"On the contrary. You might have found just the right partner for it," she said, smiling playfully. "Anyway," she said, pointing to the dress, "that one is done for now. I'm kind of tired. How long have we been at this?"

I searched for the time on the wall clock. "Three hours, give or take."

"Let's call it a day. By the way, I meant to ask you,

what company did you use to send Jen's stuff back to her? I need to move my stuff too."

"I asked Pete to drop off the boxes at her sister's. I can ask him to help you move. It's not an issue. Plus, you know you can leave stuff at my place. I'll be back so frequently that I'm not renting my place out, so your stuff will be safe."

"Are you asking me to move in," she jokingly asked.

"Well, unofficially. It just makes sense for you to leave stuff with me. Then you don't have to pay storage fees for the stuff you don't take."

"I won't crowd you?"

"Babe, have you seen the closet? You've already taken over, and I love it. The spare bedroom can be storage. It doesn't matter to me."

As I put on my regular clothes, Caroline gave me a hug. "Thank you. Thank you for everything."

"Come, let's go to dinner. It's time we have a proper drink and this fauxkale-eating, fit model needs some real food."

We walked quickly down the block with our arms linked. Caroline hadn't been this chatty or giddy since Milan. As much as she complained about the stress of her work, she was full of hope. It was one of her most endearing traits. For better or worse, she always had hope.

We were halfway through the bottle, waiting for our plates to be taken away. Caroline swirled the wine in her glass, holding it off to the side, arm crossed holding her opposite elbow. She looked at me with a sudden curiosity.

"So, what is it about..." She paused. "That stuff.

The harness and all that."

I narrowed my eyes, a little smile forming. "Whatever do you mean?" I batted my eyelashes, for which I received a huff and a wave of the hand. I chuckled as I replied, "It started as a novelty, I think. My first recollection of it was reading an article in Seventeen Magazine, back in the day, and I had been with a guy from university for a couple years. Things were getting a little stale."

"At two years? What? Did he have a dick the size of a peanut?"

I rolled my eyes. "No, it just hadn't dawned on me yet that, well, men weren't one-hundred percent my thing. So, I was trying things to compensate by exploring."

"Makes sense." Caroline leaned in toward me and whispered, "So, what did you start with?"

"The easy stuff—handcuffs, bed ties, novelties like the warming gels they sell at the drugstore." I took a sip of wine. "And you know what? It didn't help. So, I bought accessories and trashy, cliché outfits, thinking I needed to get more into the mental frame of mind, and it just didn't add any spark for me. Worked just fine for him though."

"I wish I had seen that." Caroline smirked. "Still have those?"

I leaned into her and kissed her halfway across the table. "Maybe, baby."

She smirked as she rested back into her chair. "What happened after that?"

"Usual things that happen when you're with someone you're bound to grow out of. I broke up with him after graduation and went my own way. I didn't try anything until years down the road." I took a second to think. "You know, shortly after I started exploring, it was the first time I kissed a girl."

"Threesome?"

"I wish, but no. I was with the boyfriend and his friends at a local bar. One of his friends happened to be curious, or bi—I'm not sure, it was my first time meeting her. Russian, taller than I, long black hair, heavy eye makeup, tattoos…she smoked too. Those weird, skinny cigarettes—you'd know."

"Bitch-sticks?"

I nodded. "Hmm-hmm, strawberry flavor. I remember being fascinated by her and I wanted to see what she tasted like." I let out a little giggle. "And you know me, I actually asked permission from the guy I was with to kiss her."

Caroline put down her glass and let out a huff of exasperation. "Naturally, you of all people would." She rolled her eyes.

"He said yes, but I think he regretted it almost immediately. Anyway, I had to go home to meet curfew and I wanted to kiss her so badly but didn't have the balls. Of all things, my boyfriend spoke to her in Russian and next thing I knew, she had caressed my jaw with her hand and firmly planted her lips on mine. I didn't even think about it I was so swept up in the moment. She put her tongue in my mouth and I played with her tongue piercing. I had put my hand on the small of her back, my eyes closed, wanting more. It was only when I felt a hand on my shoulder, did I come to my senses. The table of guys beside us had erupted in enthusiasm and my boyfriend was pulling me away, and that was the last time I saw her."

"That was brief, but it makes sense now."

"What does?"

"You just described a Russian Jennifer."

"Minus the Russian thing, smoking, and tongue piercing," I conceded, "but I guess their physical profiles are, or rather, were similar."

"Semantics," she said dismissively. "So, then what? Where did you go from there?"

"Back to being the girlfriend of a boyfriend."

Back to being the girlfriend to a boyfriend who now only wanted a girlfriend.

Caroline's curiosity had been peaked. "Sure, sure but after him?"

"Dated a few more guys. That guy, Tim, was the last one actually. He's into some rather creative sexual acts. He introduced me to the world of BDSM, indirectly, when he took me to a sex convention."

"I take it that doesn't stand for *Bible Discussions, Studies, and Meetings*?"

I laughed. "Not quite, smartass. I believe it stands for *bondage, dominance and submission, sadism and masochism.*"

"Where does the extra 'S' come in?"

I shrugged. "Beats me. I had to look it up when I first learned about it." Caroline had an intrigued look on her face, so I continued, "I had to do a fair amount of research about it. There's an entire spectrum of, shall we say, erotic practices, but people find niches or things that they specifically enjoy, and it grows from there."

She nodded. "I've done a little bit of research to be honest, but I didn't really know where to start. What do you like about it?"

"A variety of things, I suppose. For me, it's about

trusting my partner. It's about communicating with them, more listening than expressing for me. I apparently like to take a more controlling role."

I love taking control.

That playful expression was back on Caroline's face. "What would you do to me?"

I looked coyly at her. "You assume I would do things to you?"

"You did to Jen."

I did lots of things to Jen. Some of which I would never do to you.

I admitted, "She was curious, she seemed to enjoy, she asked for more."

"So," Caroline asked me again, "what would you do to me?"

I took her hand in mine. "Learn. I need to understand what you like, what you respond well to, and what your telltale signs are."

"How does all of this make you..." She searched for the words. "Sexually happy?"

"I'm happy if I can make you happy."

"That reeks of B.S. Fine, simpler question—how do you get off? And why don't you ever let me go down on you or at least try with my hands?"

I wanted to crawl back into my shell, but I took a sip of cabernet instead. "I don't know," I admitted. "Unless I do it, no one has accomplished that."

Caroline looked at me, alarmed. "Really? Never?"

I shrugged. "I've always assumed it's my last shred of defense and I prohibit myself."

Caroline gripped my hand a little harder. "Can I please try? Will you please just let me?"

"You might die of dehydration or tongue fatigue

first, but sure, give it a whirl," I teased. "Just, please, don't take offense if it doesn't work. I still enjoy it." I tried to recall the last time I let anyone down on me. Just the thought of it made me uncomfortable. Having finished our drinks, we ordered coffees and I asked for the bill. I texted Pete to come get us. I leaned into Caroline again. "So, you've peered into my Pandora's box. What about you?"

She shrugged. "I've never been with someone who wants to venture outside the norm."

"Vanilla," I interjected. "Norm is often called 'vanilla,' as in the most basic form of ice cream and sex."

She finished her espresso. "Sure, vanilla then. Maybe with a touch of sprinkles every once and awhile."

"Even with Sophie? She seemed like a loose cannon." I took a sip of espresso and put out my credit card.

Caroline raised her eyebrows. "She's loose all right, just not in a fun way. Drank too much even in the good days. She never really wanted to explore anything, and really, I never considered it as an option."

"Do you have any wonders now? Any fantasies?"

"Honestly, I don't know what the options are."

I walked her out of the restaurant. Pete was waiting faithfully outside, the door of the black sedan held open for us. Pete closed the car door for her, and I got in the other side.

"The possibilities are really limited to what you like or want," I said sliding a little closer to her. "What's something you've thought about?" Caroline cast her eyes down to the floor mat and mumbled something. "Say what now?" I lifted her chin to make her gaze meet mine.

"You'll judge."

"Repeating the wise words my best friend told me not too long ago, 'we're way past judgement.' And like I just said, this is about trust."

Buckling up, Caroline twitched her nose, and turned to me. "Bondage, maybe?"

How cute.

I kissed her temple. "We can try that." I brought her into my shoulder, and she rested her head heavily. I kissed the top of her hair, breathing in her scent. "Caroline?" She looked up at me, radiant green eyes staring deeply into mine. I couldn't bring myself to tell her, my mouth didn't open, scared to divulge too much. I kissed her lips deeply instead. I hoped in some way she would understand. Pitifully, all I could muster was a "thank you."

I love you.

She smiled innocently, returning a second kiss.

Chapter Ten

"Thanks for driving me." Caroline fiddled with her passport, looking down into her lap.

"Of course." I held her hand, trying to make the moment last.

"I guess…"

"Yea, I know." I opened the car door as the frigid air smacked my face. I opened the car trunk, lifting her suitcase out.

Caroline crept out of the car and stood before me. Her eyes were watering. "What the hell?" She shook her head. "What did you do to me?"

I took her in my arms. "I know. I'll miss you too." I held her tightly. "I'll see you soon."

"You better." She looked up at me. "But you know what? Fuck you." The corners of her mouth lifted a little.

"I wish." I lowered my voice to a whisper. "Why?"

"Don't play dumb. You know."

Just tell her already, you idiot.

I kissed her, taking her into my arms. I felt like she was leaving me for an eternity. "I know."

"See you," she said, reluctantly wheeling her bag behind her. She walked painfully slowly to the airport doors, taking a look back at me.

I waved, opening the car door.

What am I doing?

I shut the car door again, abruptly, and ran over to her, taking her in my arms and lifting her small frame almost off the ground. I buried my face into the flurry of her hair. I could feel my eyes watering.

I love you.

Caroline hugged me tighter. "I know."

I kissed her passionately one last time and let her walk away. I got back into my car and sped away, seemingly trying to run from my own mix of emotions.

I love her, so why can't I tell her? Why am I so scared to let myself open up to her and trust her? Why can't I just confess? I love her more than anyone I have ever been with...more than I could ever be with anyone else. I want her in my life, always. What the hell happened? What did she do to me? Why did I fall in love? I promised myself I wouldn't. I shouldn't. These things never work out well. But I want it to.

****

That night I stared at the ceiling, imagining Caroline beside me, her warmth radiating between my thighs as she straddles one leg. I picture flipping her over, her beautiful body anticipating my touch. I envisioned kissing her perfectly soft lips, licking her neck, traveling down to her breasts, working my lips farther to her belly button, teasing her pelvis as I ran my fingers over her underwear, flirting with her clit.

I slid my hand under the band of my thong, continuing my Caroline dream. The sheets still smelled like her. I felt my own breast, imagining her fingers gripping my nipple and pinching lightheartedly. I slid a finger between the lips of my pussy as if it were her tongue. I wondered if I could let her kissable tongue dance between them. My memory was vivid, recanting the recent memories. I was wet for her. I played with my clit a little more enthusiastically, encouraging a tingling heat.

I changed mental scenes to see Caroline on her back, clutching the pillow above her head, eyes closed, awaiting her release as I worked my tongue around her clit. I brought myself to the edge, hearing Caroline moan as she grasped the pillow tighter. I let myself cum while I pictured Caroline's back arched in pleasure as her legs fell open, letting me in deeper. She gasped, swearing softly. I held the image in my head, extending my orgasm a little longer.

I relaxed back into the mattress, opening my eyes with nothing but the darkness to welcome me. It was going to be a long few weeks.

****

We spoke every day, multiple times per day. I was exhausted from exceptionally early morning calls to review Caroline's latest design inspirations. Francesco wanted the buy-in of some of his corporate Italian contacts before the launch, stressing Caroline beyond an acceptable level. Although a week early, I had talked to Georgi that Monday and asked to finish the yearly company wrap-up abroad. I had completed the annual review weeks in advance, as I usually did, so he didn't seem to have much of a problem with my request.

The deal was that I would keep working for Georgi on the side since, apparently, I was the only one who made a successful marketing campaign that exceeded the return on financial investment by five-fold. He wasn't ready to let that go. Francesco had agreed without any hesitation. Regardless if they were both wearing rose-colored glasses or not, I signed the mutual non-disclosure and became a team member of Caroline's dedicated crew while maintaining a hand at Georgi's design studio. It was going to be more work than I had time for, but I would make it work somehow.

Placing a box of Caroline's favorite candies in my bag, I zipped up my checked luggage and took one last look around the apartment. It would be a month or so until I came back, and I was more than ready for a change. Ready to run from the cold of Toronto, the lingering memories of Jen, and head for the moderate warmth of Milan and Caroline's arms. I left a note with the concierge for the cleaning staff, who I had booked to arrive in advance of my return. I didn't want to come back to a dusty apartment. With Pete's help, I was off to the airport quickly.

I hadn't told Caroline I was coming early, figuring it would be a nice surprise. The image of Jen sitting on the kitchen counter with Christine between her legs flashed in my head. Either Caroline would be thrilled of my early arrival, or I'd find myself getting a different hotel room. But I could trust Caroline. She wouldn't do that to me. I hoped.

I slept most of the flight and worked the rest, arriving in Milan just before dinner. I hurriedly took a taxi to the hotel. I knew Caroline had planned to meet up with some of her colleagues that night and I hoped she hadn't left already.

Although with a room key, I knocked on her hotel door. No answer. I knocked again, sliding the room key. "Turn down service," I called out. I was met with silence.

The room was pitch black and I could smell the faint aroma of cherry smoke in the air. This was definitely the right room. I flicked on the lights, dragging my luggage through the door. No one was home.

Caroline's things were neatly organized on the dresser, clothes hung up in her version of black coordination, and shoes lined up perfectly against the wall. I unzipped my bag and brought out a new set of clothes and my toiletry bag. I couldn't go join them for dinner like this. I opened the bathroom door and was greeted by a lacy, black teddy hanging on the shower wall. There were no tags hanging on it. Examining it a little more closely, I could feel that its satin elements were still a little damp.

It looks new but it's been washed. Caroline doesn't wear these out of the house. Why?

I could feel my heart thudding harder in my chest, a pang of betrayal settling in my lungs as I breathed deeply, trying to remain calm. I could feel my eyes starting to burn with tears.

I'm sure she has a reason. She isn't like the others. Caroline is not Jen.

I could hear the hotel door unlock and a spry voice called out, "Housekeeping! Miss, I have the extra towels you ordered." I came around the bathroom corner to be face to face with an absolutely stunning brunette, her uniform shirt unbuttoned a little, exposing the top of her cleavage. Her charmingly flirtatious smile quickly wiped off her face as soon as she saw me. I was definitely not who she was expecting.

I reached out for the towels. "Thanks, I'll take those."

She nodded and did a little bow with her head as she walked quickly, partially backwards, and headed to the door. "Is there anything I can get you and Ms…"

"We're fine, thank you," I replied with a forced smile. I couldn't help but shut the door rather abruptly. I took a glance over my shoulder at the teddy hanging conspicuously in the bathroom.

What was that? How will I handle this? Benefit of the doubt? If nothing else, Caroline always had great taste. I can see the allure…

My phone buzzed in my pocket. It was Caroline.

—*Lover! How are you? I haven't heard from you in a while. How was your day? Facetime tonight?*—

Deep breathe. Be cool. I texted her back.

—*Hey babe, all good with me. Sorry, just busy today. How are you? You out for dinner at some place fantastic?*—

—*Left a little while ago. At this place I think you'd like. Something called La Parisienne. We're just about to eat.*—

I had to say something.

—*Bon Appetit! And, yes, lets chat tonight.*—

—*XOXO*—

Nothing abnormal.

I Googled the restaurant and finished changing into something a little fiercer than planned. The teddy issue would have to wait. I got into a cab and, five minutes out, I called her up.

"Hello?"

"Hey babe, just me."

"Hey! Sorry, it's loud in here. Let me just go outside. One sec."

The taxi rounded the corner and I started looking for her as I paid the fare. My heart was racing. I was so happy, so excited, so worried, so in love I didn't know what to do. I started walking down the street toward the restaurant. I spotted her, black fur clutched around her shoulders, leaning against the patio railing, rummaging through her purse for her light.

Caroline continued, "Hey, okay, I'm outside. Sorry about that. How are you? I miss you so much!" I could see her radiating smile from half a block up.

At least she's happy to talk to me.

"I miss you too. So, babe, I was wondering..." I quickened my steps, trying to muffle the sound of my heels on the sidewalk. "How you would feel..." I paused, trying to walk faster than the words could be spoken.

"Feel about what?" She blew a stream of smoke into the air.

I was five strides away. Still holding the phone but within earshot, I said, "If I came a little earlier than planned." Caroline almost dropped her vape as she saw me and threw her arms around my neck. She peppered my lips with kisses, and I hugged her harder.

"Oh my God, I missed you so much! I can't believe you're here!" She was exuberant, smiling ear to ear.

I buried my face into her hair. "So, I guess I should head back? Be on the next plane home?"

"Shut up," she muttered. She nuzzled into my neck.

"I missed you too." I breathed in the scent of her shampoo, letting the familiar smell bring me additional comfort. "I went to the hotel hoping to catch you but, obviously you had already left." I took a marginal step back, taking in the beauty of her green eyes. They caught the light of the streetlamps, somehow managing to add even more allure.

She looped arms with me and pulled me closer to

her. Looking up at the night sky, she smiled. "Thank you for coming early." She looked back toward me. "All of this is really stressing me out."

I kissed her head. "I know. I'm here for you, and this way, you won't call me at five in the morning to ask me what kind of edge stitch you should use. It's not like you even use what I suggest."

She laughed. "Well, you're making progress. When I first met you, you had no idea what an edge stitch was or that there are different kinds."

We headed back inside, and I managed to keep it together for the rest of the night, partially distracted by all the new faces on her hand-picked team, and partially from Francesco's constant high-pitch giggle that erupted at the end of the table. It wasn't until we got into the taxi back that my stomach sunk to the floor. I was quiet the whole time, letting Caroline chat about the latest group gossip she had overheard from Francesco. I slid the key card into the door and put on a brave smile. She slipped by me without hesitation.

Caroline took off her heels, burying her feet into the area rug. I hung up our jackets as she wrapped her arms around me from behind.

I turned to face her and kissed her forehead. "I'll be right back." I needed to get this off my chest. I headed in the direction of the bathroom.

Caroline grabbed my wrist. "Wait. One second." She trotted off to the bathroom and shut the door.

I decided to wait, fully clothed, perched on the edge of the bed. I fiddled with the rings on my fingers. She emerged a couple minutes later, her beautiful, sleek body hugged tightly by the lace teddy.

"What do you think?" She did a little twirl.

Damn, how could I ever be mad at her? She's too cute.

The fabric held her ass daringly in place, her breasts perky and inviting. It had a hint of girl-next-door meets dominatrix. "I bought it yesterday. It was on sale because it had some weird stain. Not a white stain so I figured it was safe." She ran her hands down the sides of her torso. "But it was just so...I washed it and...you're silent. You hate it? I knew it." She cast her gaze to the floor. "Why? What's wrong with it?" I could see her shutting down further as she continued, "I tried...I want to be what you want..." Her voice trailed off.

A weight lifted off my chest and I took a deep breath, kicking off my shoes and letting a small smile creep across my face.

I'm being ridiculous. This is Caroline. I can do this.

I motioned for her to come to me, uncrossing my legs for her to stand between them. I ran my fingers under the lace edges, gripping her ass cheeks gently in each hand. I smiled more broadly at her concerned face. "You look amazing in it. Absolutely stunning. And you know what?" Her shoulders had curled inwards, trying to hide in plain sight. She shrugged. "You *are* what I want. You are so much more than I deserve. You are more than I could have ever even dreamed of. I had no idea what we have even existed."

She pouted like a little girl who dropped her ice cream on the ground. "Sure, sure."

I love this girl more than I could love anyone else.

"Caroline, look at me." Her green eyes were an emerald color in the room's dimmed light. "Don't you know that I love you? I love you more than life itself."

"You do?" She ran her fingers through my hair, searching in my eyes for the truth she had always strived to obtain. A truth she could hold onto.

I brought her closer into my arms, maintaining eye contact. "I love you, Caroline."

She leaned down a little, holding my face in her palms, placing a tender kiss on my lips. "I've always loved you."

Chapter Eleven

I had been in Milan with Caroline for over a month now. Christmas had long come and gone, New Years was a blur, and we had finally settled into the company-provided apartment in Brera. I walked out the courtyard door, stepping into the bustle of the street. I could see my breath as I trotted quickly down the cobblestone path, envying the people and their blanket-laden Vespa's. I checked my phone's map app as I navigated through the streets. I was headed to an erotic store near Simonetta, a brisk thirty-minute walk away.

Caroline kept hinting at her interest in bondage and I was willing to comply. I was a little anxious about bringing her into the world of BDSM, much more nervous than I had been with Jen. Jen delved into it like it was something she had always done, and she became the submissive she thought I wanted. I tried to envision Caroline like that, and I found it challenging. Perhaps because our relationship had grown from friendship rather than sheer physical chemistry, but we were in such a good place, I didn't want to take a chance and compromise that.

My steps quickened as I approached the store—a black and pink awning with a basic silhouette of a woman's figure hung overhead. The store was lined with the usual suspects of items—frilly outfits, sexy lingerie, vibrators, dildos, videos, and a large variety of lubricants. I saw a hanging sign above a staircase to the basement level. "Kink" it read, in bold black letters. I walked below the sign, down the flight of stairs, and was greeted with what I had been looking for.

Like many countries, there were certain culturally prominent sexual interests amongst locals, and in Italy, bondage was one of the more favored activities, which was lucky for me. The walls were well stocked with whips, floggers, chains, cuffs, ropes, and plexiglass displays of nipple clamps, anal plugs, and things I couldn't even decipher the use for. I ran my fingers over some silk, Japanese rope, selecting one five-meter, black spool and another two-meter length. I couldn't help but pick out a bed restraint kit as well. It always seemed to come in handy.

I was careful about the collar and wrist restraints, making sure the leathers were soft and the buckles well-padded from the skin. Everything to match. I chose a set of black with gold hardware. I elected for a black, satin blindfold with self-ties.

I moved to the anal plugs, looking for a small, silicone starter plug. Having left most of my leathers, hardware, and miscellaneous supplies back home and, having shipped Jen the silicone toys I used with her, I took the liberty of buying myself one of my favorites, an inflatable anal pump. After I grabbed a set of Kegel balls, a couple bottles of lubricants, and some toy cleaner, I was still missing a couple essentials. I left my weighty basket of paraphernalia at the unmanned lower register counter and went to browse the selection of attire.

Corsets, harnesses, and garters were by the multiple. I needed one to speak to me but, more importantly, I needed to know Caroline would want to essentially rip it off me. I found one in my size that was definitely dominatrix enough. I grabbed the matching garter and went to the change room. By now, I could do up a corset in the dark or with my eyes closed. I laced it tightly against my ribcage—it pushed my breasts up tantalizingly. Brass studs adorned the ribbing and trimmed the top of the neckline. It curved just slightly over my hips where buckles then attached to the garter's straps.

I snapped a photo of it in the mirror, slanted enough to cut out sixty percent but exposing enough to be enticing. I sent it to her.

—Like?—

I got dressed and took another sweep of the floor. I was looking at a feather tickler when she responded.

—Damn, you're such a tease.—

—So, that's a no?—

—Please, please get it. Please.—

—I'm not convinced, you'll have to show me how much you like it later tonight.—

Adding the jewel encrusted tickler and a coordinating whip to my pile, I went to the check out. I left the store with three nondescript black shopping bags in hand. My phone rang as I made my way back to the apartment.

"When do I get to see that on you?"

I giggled at her eagerness. "Tonight, maybe."

"Not earlier? I'm almost done with the fittings here."

"Have you eaten yet?"

"I could eat you for lunch," she confessed, "but no, I'm starving. My assistant forgot to bring me breakfast like I had asked."

"Let's go to that little trattoria we went to last Sunday for brunch. The one on Via Santa Marta. I can meet you there in forty minutes, if that works for you?"

"Sounds good. See you then."

I rushed to walk the rest of the way, dropping off almost all the packages back at the apartment. I tucked the satin bag of Kegel balls in my jacket pocket and made my way to the restaurant. Caroline texted that she was a few minutes behind. I decided to wait at the table for her as it was too cold to wait outside. I saw her walk in a couple minutes later.

Wow.

She was stunning without even trying. Her luscious hair moved back from her face as the door heater blew onto her. She walked through the second set of doors. Wearing a khaki coat, dark gray jeans, and black boots, it was nothing out of the ordinary, but she was stunning all the same. Caroline had an air about her that just radiated self-assurance and a genuine personality. The host greeted her warmly and she responded politely. Caroline was motioned in my direction and her face lit up. I stood to greet her.

"*Ciao, ciao.*" I kissed her a little more passionately than I had intended, letting the kiss linger. I felt the corners of her mouth turn upward.

"*Ciao, mi amore,*" she replied, sitting down and removing her coat. "So, what *exactly* have you been up to?" Her eyebrow raised provocatively.

"Shouldn't we order wine first before we get into all this?"

A cheeky smile formed on her face. "This is why I love Europe. You can have wine in the middle of the day, and you are spared judgement."

"You and me both." I motioned for the server and ordered a half bottle of house vino with a couple appetizers for us to snack on. "I found a couple things I think you might like to explore today."

"Is that so?" Caroline popped an olive in her mouth. "Like what?"

"Babe, you know I'm hesitant to do any of this. I love you and I don't want you to be doing this just for me, as sweet as that is."

She rolled her eyes at me. "Oh stop. You should know by now that I'm at the very least curious. Just show me."

I wasn't going to give up my prodding that easily. "Well, you say you're curious about bondage, so, what about it entices you?"

Caroline took a sip of wine as she contemplated her answer. "The feeling of exposure I suppose. I have never trusted someone enough to let my guard down like that. I guess I want to see if I like it."

"And you trust me enough to do that?"

She shrugged a little. "I trust you more than anyone I have ever been with, so, yes."

"What else? What have you tried?" Caroline blushed pink and I couldn't help but smile.

"You love asking me these things in public, don't you?" Caroline took another sip.

I shrugged lightly. "Why not? Seems like a great time to talk about it." My lips formed a mischievous smile.

She rolled her eyes. "Well," she started, "with Sophie, she wanted me to be the more dominating one. I don't think I ever got the hang of that. I more or less felt like her toy more than her lover. She was such a damn handful that one."

I puckered my lips slightly. "What did you try beyond the vanilla?"

Caroline's voice lowered in volume a little. "Anal was pretty big for her but I hardly ever received and when I did, she was too impatient with a strap-on." Caroline paused, her face cringing a bit at the memory. "We tried handcuffs once, about the same time when I could sense her eyes were straying beyond me, but that didn't really end well. I even entertained a threesome with her and another girl, but we all know how that ended up." Caroline rolled her eyes, fidgeting with her glass.

I swirled the remaining liquid in my glass. "So, what do you want from me? You want to try bondage, sure, but what emotional or mental response are you trying to provoke?"

"From you?" She took a moment. "I guess I want to learn what you want. We already have great chemistry. I'm curious as to what you enjoy. I want to be the first one to actually make you orgasm." I rolled my eyes slightly as she continued, "I want to learn not to overthink and just enjoy the moment."

"You think me dominating you will help?" I let the question linger in the air as she searched for an answer.

"Perhaps." She cast her gaze down shyly. "I'm open to learning."

"I must confess," I continued, knowing full well the risk of exposing myself, "you are the first person I have truly loved. That said, I really doubt that I will be able to be one hundred percent Dominant. I won't be able to let my emotions fall to the side."

"Are you at all curious?"

I smiled with a little defiance. "I want to learn your boundaries. Push them a little."

"Or a lot," she responded playfully as she held my gaze. "So, tell me, what did you find today?"

The corners of my mouth turned upward coyly, "I picked up a few things I think you might like, but I have one that I'd like you to try now, if you don't mind."

"Now?" Caroline's eyes widened.

"Hmm-hmm." I nodded and handed her the little black pouch from my pocket. "These are Kegel balls. They go inside. I'd hold them for a little bit, they're a bit cold."

Caroline held them in her palm. "What do they do?"

"Theoretically, they strengthen your pelvic floor muscles. Takes about a month or so but should essentially heighten your orgasm."

She smiled. "Like I need that with you."

"Go." I motioned to the bathroom with my hand. "Try them."

Caroline kept her palm clutched as she walked to the bathroom. She came back a few minutes later. "I should have held them longer. Those things are cold!"

I laughed. "They'll be warm soon enough."

Caroline paused, letting her thoughts brew. "Can I ask you something?"

"Of course. Anything." I took a sip, putting my glass back on the table and carefully attempting to dissipate any visible effects of the alcohol racing through my blood stream.

"Did you love her?" She shifted in her seat. "Her,

as in Jen."

A little uncomfortable at the mention of my ex, I looked down at my hand on the stem of my glass. "I think at the time I thought I might have, but it always felt wrong. I was always trying so hard to make things work." I took a pause. "Honestly, I don't think she was ever truly happy with me. Maybe I was compensating for it. At least, I was trying to."

"She was your Sophie."

I looked at her a bit puzzled. "How so?"

"Troubled, acted out, demanded attention, needy." She tilted her head as she played with the rim of her glass. "Sound familiar? You tried to fix things, you made the time, made the effort, and it was never enough."

I nodded. I felt my eyes starting to water and I looked away, fixing my gaze on the wall painting behind her.

"My love," she continued, "she's spilt milk, not worth crying over. You did your best. Do you remember what you told me when things with Sophie went sour, time and time again? You said I had given my heart to someone who didn't really want or appreciate it. Jen won't ever be happy. Look at how she tried to get back at you for simply having a photo taken with me?"

I looked at her sympathetic eyes. "I'm scared. What will happen to us in a couple years? Will we be like what we've both been through?"

Caroline reached for my hand. "No, my love, we will not be. You know why I say that? We've started this off as best friends. You've helped me through many tough times, and hopefully I've been there enough for you. You've seen me with my mascara running down my face. I've seen you cry…come to think of it, I've only seen you cry once." She waved her hand dismissively. "Still counts. My point is, we've been through a lot together and we've done pretty well."

"I think we have the physical thing down too." I offered a little smile.

Caroline rose out of her seat and grasped my face in her hands, kissing me firmly. "I love you and don't you forget it." She paused. "Damn it, one of my Kegel balls just fell out."

We both burst out laughing.

"Thank God for jeans," Caroline whispered, her eyes playful.

Chapter Twelve

The crowd rose to their feet in applause as Caroline's debut show came to an end. The girls were doing their final catwalk as she took a shy bow and clapped herself out of view, trailing the last few models. She scanned the crowd for me backstage as she came off the stage ledge.

Caroline threw her arms around my neck. "I can't believe it, I just opened for Valentino." Her face was flush with excitement.

"They loved it. Congratulations, babe." I kissed her deeply. "I'm so proud of you."

She sighed nervously. "I hope so, but I won't really know till the critics publish. Did you see Anna Winters make any facial signs of approval?"

"I couldn't really see, but honestly, it doesn't matter." It was a white lie—the Editor in Chief of the top fashion magazine, Bella Vita, hadn't moved a facial muscle, or made a peep to her acquaintances, and her review would have an enormous impact on Caroline's career. "This is about you building your dream," I mustered to say as we were ushered out of the way for the main show. Caroline trotted off to take care of her prime photo opportunities as I stood off to the side, making sure to stay out of the limelight. I felt a presence behind me. It made me uncomfortable.

"You must be so proud of our Caroline." I could

hear her familiar voice sneer from behind.

I turned my head. I already wanted to react defensively, but I held my tongue. "Yes, Sophie, I'm very proud of Caroline, as I'm sure you are as well."

I can't stand you. Why do you feel so compelled to talk to me?

"I saw your photo in the Times—very cute. It seems you two are off to a good start." Sophie continued in her condescending tone. "From what I've heard, you'll be too much for her so let me know when you're free again."

I looked at her with a little alarm, a severe degree of annoyance in my voice. "What on earth are you talking about?"

Sophie laughed, holding a smirk on her face. "Don't you know that Jen and I have become good 'friends' since you tossed her aside." The sarcasm dripped off her tongue like venom. "I've heard so much about how you handle your *pets*, and...you know what?" She leaned in, almost touching her lips to my ear. "I would have enjoyed a good fuck from you more than that inexperienced prude, and you'll be more than Carol can handle. I'm sure I'll hear it through the vine, but you can come play Mistress with me when you're done playing house with her."

Great. Fantastic news. How exactly did she and Jen get together?

I stared ahead, focusing on nothing, too bewildered, shocked and at a loss for words. I felt Caroline nearby, probably now seeing the situation unfolding before her. I gathered my senses, picked my figurative jaw up off the floor, and looked at Sophie straight in the eye, "I love Caroline, and we would both appreciate it if you left us alone."

"Mark my words." She tapped her lips with her finger. "You'll get bored of screwing her and want someone who wants her hair pulled and a fist full..."

Just shut up.

I walked away before she could finish her sentence.

Caroline, doe-eyed, came up beside me. "What was that all about? You seem upset. Why is she backstage?"

I forced a smile. "Who knows? All I know for sure is...I'm really happy you left her." I grabbed her hand. "Let's go. We have a party to get to. It's time to celebrate."

We went to her private dressing room at the back of the studio. The door shut behind us muffling the sound of the crowd and music. I did my best to let the encounter with Sophie go, watching Caroline undo her hair. It flowed voluptuously over her shoulders. I couldn't help but smile at her beauty.

"It'll be flooded with Press," she said, touching up her mascara and looking at me indirectly in the mirror. "I was wondering how you would feel about wearing something coordinated. I want to set the right tone."

"Yea, of course. What did you have in mind?"

Caroline had set aside a couple options for the after party. She motioned to the rack. "Pull the black and gold sequined dresses. Black for me if you don't mind. I brought you black stilettos, I'll wear the red."

"I haven't seen these before. They're amazing." I began to remove my existing dress.

"I made them a few nights ago. Not too much? Yours has a full back, don't worry. I know I can't get you to go braless unless I forcefully remove it." She glanced at me flirtatiously.

"My boobs aren't perfect and perky like yours," I retorted, "so not fair!"

"I may be older but you're bigger than me, babe." She blew a kiss at me. "And I love it."

Pulling my dress off, I took the time to admire the gold mini dress hanging on the end of the rack. Its full-length sleeves had been embellished with larger rhinestones while the length of the sleeve was trimmed with black accents. Its neck formed a modest but intriguing V. It hugged all the right places.

"Hmm-hmm, you look delicious in that." She grabbed my ass. "I do a damn fine job sometimes." She finished pinning up her loosely curled hair and put her dress on too. They were almost duplicates, but Caroline had opted for a very conservative neckline and plunging back complete with a gold and silver accent chain dangling down her spine.

I slid my hand around her exposed back, making my way to her waist. I turned her, so we stood side-by-side and faced the floor to ceiling mirror. What stared back was a couple to be reckoned with. "Think this will set the right tone?" I gripped her waist a little tighter, pulling her toward me.

We look amazing together.

"It's perfect. It's us," she said, fiddling with her bracelets.

I eyed the lines of her body in the dress, craving her already. "I could do so many naughty things to you," I whispered in her ear.

She met my eyes in the mirror. "Like what?" The corners of her mouth lifted playfully.

I kissed her cheek, bringing her hands forward to rest on the table. She leaned over, pushing her ass out. I continued to caress her neck, sliding my fingers along her spine, feeling the softness of her skin. The hem of her dress barely covered her assets. Caroline closed her eyes, breathing deeply, enjoying the sensations of my fingers running down the back of her thighs. I let my hands brush upward between her legs. A little shiver ran down her spine as I caressed her in my hand, adding pressure to her clit. I rubbed ever so gently, and she looked at me from the corner of her eye.

"Tease," she accused playfully.

I dared her to contradict me further. My eyes held steady with hers as I held my hand firmly, rubbing her clit purposefully. I slipped a finger into her thong, feeling her wetness.

Keeping her eyes closed, she moaned, "You know we have to go."

I let my fingers provoke the notion of entering her fully. Gently removing my hand from her now damp thong, I kissed her shoulder. "If you insist." I spanked her ass lightly as I grabbed my phone and purse off the table.

Caroline mumbled under breath, "I don't have any extra underwear." Her mouth formed into a cute, child-like pout.

"You don't really need to wear any." I cocked my head at her provocatively.

****

We walked into the bar lounge and it was already packed. Caroline and I flashed our passes to get into the VIP area. Everyone was there. I let Caroline lead as we navigated the crowd. We ended up at a table near the back, surrounded by Caroline's models and team. I saw Francesco with his hand on the upper thigh of his latest amusement at the cube table next to us. Judging by his body language he was already a few drinks in, but he managed a wave in our direction.

Not a fan of pre-ordered, pre-distributed drinks, I asked for a glass of cabernet and ordered Caroline a fresh vodka, soda, cranberry with a wedge of lime. I had my arm around her, leaning against the back of the couch, as Caroline chatted with the many, many people that came by with congratulatory words. I piped in a '*ciao*' or friendly smile when Caroline patted my knee to acknowledge the patron but for the most part, I surveyed the crowd.

There were a ton of eccentrics, wearing anything they thought would warrant attention. Then there were the judgmental people, like myself, sitting or perching themselves around the outskirts, predominantly wearing black and clearly making snide remarks to a friend when someone walked by. The remainder of the guests were a mix of celebrities that were already bored by the night's events, some who were too drunk having fun, a very select few behaving themselves, and a smaller amount still on their way to stardom.

I rubbed Caroline's bare back. My touch was cool on her skin and it made her jump a little and giggle. She turned to kiss me. I melted at the slightest touch of her flawlessly rouged lips. It was a moment, perfect on its own, her strawberry-blonde hair flowing effortlessly over her shoulders. Her smile was radiant, projecting happiness. I met her sparkling eyes and couldn't help but return the smile.

I love her eyes. I love her hair. I love her.

I moved a piece of her hair behind her ear, encouraging her to lean into me as our noses touched tips. I froze those twenty seconds, wanting to remember the memory in its preciseness. We broke from our moment as Francesco came to make rather drunk conversation. He was brief about it as his partner dragged him to the dance floor. My gaze followed them to the floor where my eyes unfortunately met with Sophie's. She smirked. She twirled the girl she was with.

Please don't let it be...

Of course, it was Jen.

Fuck me.

I looked at Caroline abruptly. Obviously seeing the same situation unfold as I had, she looked back at me in horror and with a twang of confusion. In an attempt to take the figurative 'high road' I changed my tone, shrugged, and shook my head, trying to keep my face relatively neutral. I put my hand on her shoulder and pulled her into me, kissing the top of her head.

"They can only bother us as much as we let them," I whispered into her ear.

She nodded and looked up into my eyes, her green eyes so trusting, placing a tender kiss on my lips.

As Caroline's lips left mine, I felt an aggressive tug on my arm. Sophie stood a few feet away, watching the situation unfold as Jen yanked on my arm again. Caroline extended her hand to try and keep distance between me and a furiously angry Jen. I stood, sheltering Caroline behind me. Jen screamed viciously over the music, slurring her words as she spat words in disdain. The music was loud and drowning. I held my free hand up in front of my chest, trying to diffuse the situation. Jen wasn't about to back down, throwing the remainder of her drink at me. She had already finished the contents, so an olive was all that hit me. Jen inched closer, gesturing wildly, frantically pointing at Caroline, still yelling. She threw her emptied glass on the floor, shattering it. The commotion had already caught security's attention, with five robustly built men appearing suddenly from the crowd. I still had my hands up in defense, Caroline stood behind me with a hand on my back. I looked for Caroline's ex in the crowd. She apparently had pulled a Houdini, disappearing into the mass of people, disowning her convenience-only-girlfriend.

Security struggled to get a hold on Jen, who had very little regard for their presence. Two men pulled her away from us, taking her by her forearms out the back door of the room. She still screamed over her shoulder, stumbling over her own shoes.

I squeezed Caroline's hand. It was time to call it a night.

Chapter Thirteen

I woke up with a slight headache to the sound of my phone buzzing on the bedside table. It was a local number but with no caller ID. I groggily answered, "Hello? I mean…"—clearing my throat—"*Pronto*?" I sat up in bed a little more.

"*Buongiorno*, is this Ms. Jones?"

"It is. Who may I ask is calling?"

"This is Commissario Romano with the Milan Polizia. We have you as the contact number for a Ms. Jennifer Blanche. I'm afraid we need to ask you to come collect Ms. Blanche from our station."

I shook my head, sighing. "Has she been charged with anything?"

"Public intoxication, whereby the fine for a first-time offense is one-hundred Euros. She will be discharged at eleven o'clock this morning with payment due at that time. Ms. Blanche claims she is unable to provide payment. Will you be able to make the appropriate arrangements?"

Caroline rolled over in bed to stare at me. I rolled my eyes. "Yes, thank you, officer. I will arrange accordingly." I hung up and let the phone fall into my lap.

"What happened?" Caroline's sleepy eyes barely opened.

I sighed. "Jen got herself arrested for public

intoxication. She spent the night in the drunk tank and rung up a one-hundred Euro fine."

Caroline squinted against the light, perching herself up on an elbow. "Why did they call you? She's here with Sophie."

"Apparently, I'm still her go-to contact. Plus, do you really think Sophie would stick around to deal with the mess she made?" I shrugged. "I have to go get her at eleven when they let her out and pay the fine since apparently Jen doesn't have the means."

"That's pretty screwed up." Caroline flopped back into her pillow and stared at the ceiling. "Do you ever wonder how we ended up respectively dating those two?"

"All the time." I sighed. "I better go shower and get ready. Do you want to come with me on this lovely errand?"

Caroline snorted. "I'd rather have my eyes pecked out by the crows." She pulled the covers over her shoulders. "But you have an excellent time. Call me once you've been relieved of your duties."

****

I walked up to the station's receptionist and provided my details and credit card, paying Jen's fine. It wasn't long before a very disheveled Jen walked through the door clutching her heels and purse. She was wearing the same red dress I had given her months before, now ruined with stains. Her hair was oily and pulled back into a sleek ponytail. She didn't meet my eyes with hers. I handed her the extra pair of flat shoes I had brought. She accepted them silently, removing the foam flip flops they had provided her.

I opened the station door, letting Jen step back to

freedom. "Where are you staying?"

She murmured under her breath, "I was staying with Sophie. I haven't been able to reach her."

"I figured that would be the case. So, what hotel?"

"Leone Reale."

I raised my eyebrows—of course Sophie would try and 'wow' Jen to get the buy-in. I hailed a cab and we made the silent journey to the Leone Reale. It was an excruciatingly long twenty minutes.

"I don't have the room key anymore." Jen's voice was muffled as we walked toward the hotel doors.

I sighed as I walked up to the hotel counter with Jen's ID, trying to explain the situation with as little detail as possible. Walking into the room, it was evident that Sophie was long gone. I noted a notecard on the table had been placed rather carelessly under an open wine bottle, which had stained the vast majority of the paper.

Jen walked to the bathroom to wash her face as I waited by the window, watching passersby below. She came back dressed in the hotel robe and slippers.

"Here," she said, handing me my shoes back, "thank you for those."

I nodded and pointed. "There's a note card on the dresser for you." Jen read it and threw it back down.

"Sophie had to take off to London unexpectedly." Jen sat on the edge of the bed facing away from me, holding her face in her hands, and began to sob. I caved and sat beside her, wrapping an arm around her shoulders.

Mascara streaming down her face, Jen whimpered, "She was just using me to get to you and Carol, wasn't she?"

"Seems that way," I said softly, feeling the slightest pang of pity for her. She reminded me so much of a high school girl who had just been dumped by her crush.

But that doesn't give you any excuse.

"I'm sorry. I was just so angry." She looked at me with puffy eyes. "I didn't mean to do…" She waved her arm in a circle. "This, or hurt you."

I pursed my lips, wondering whether or not to bite my tongue. "Yes, you meant to hurt me," I corrected her. "I'm pretty sure you wanted to participate in Sophie's vendetta to hurt Carol and knew you would be actively hurting me in the process."

Jen looked at me sharply, the teary 'woe-is-me' look swiftly gone. I let my arm drop to the bed.

Her face contorted with anger. "You pissed me off. You were basically throwing your relationship with Carol in my face with that Times release. I wasn't going to let you walk all over me."

I smiled to myself. Seeing her bipolar reaction made any twinge of compassion disappear. "I realize it angered you, and I apologize that I didn't have time to warn you before it came out, but that photo was from the release night for her clothing line. I work with her, there was nothing romantic about that photo. Everything between us happened after that photo was taken. I didn't want to tell you over the phone. I at least wanted to discuss it in person." I stayed silent for a while as I contemplated mentioning the Christine kitchen incident. I held off.

Take the high road.

I continued softly, "We've known each other for over a year so you know how upfront I am about things.

If there was something going on between Carol and me before, I would have told you and we would have ended things as amicably as possible." I sighed. "Regardless, all of this is a mess. It's an unnecessary mess. We could have just talked through it."

Jen looked at me, still angry, but now also visibly worried. "Does an arrest in Italy show back home?"

I shrugged. "You're better off asking a lawyer. I have no idea." I collected myself off the bed and started for the door, double checking to make sure I didn't leave anything behind.

Crossing her arms, Jen asked, "I guess I should say sorry?"

I half smiled at her insincerity. "Only if you mean it."

Jen shrugged. "I guess. I owe you a hundred Euros, don't I?"

I waived dismissively at the offer. "Don't worry about it. Consider it a parting token. I'm going to go now, Jen." I held back any other comments that were so daringly resting on the tip of my tongue. "I hope you have a safe journey back home."

She fished for her phone. "I'll transfer you the…"

"Don't worry about it." I started moving toward the door. "Look after yourself." I looked back at her with a little disappointment. "Oh, and Jennifer?"

"Hmm? What?"

I opened the door, ready to swiftly make an exit. "Change the number of your emergency contact." I let the door shut behind me but not before I heard her swear under her breath.

I walked quickly down the hall of the hotel, almost running for the elevator. It was the first time I had finally felt liberated from the Jen situation. Stepping out of the hotel I rang Caroline to meet for lunch at one of our favorite places. Deciding to walk, I put my headphones on and smiled a little. There was such a weight lifted, one that I hadn't even noticed I was carrying. There was a spring in my step again.

I saw Caroline waiting for me on the pedestrian roadway and I wrapped my arms around her from behind. Picking her off the ground just a little, I kissed the back of her ear.

Caroline laughed a little. "Wow, someone is happy. What happened?"

I couldn't help but grin. "I love you."

"I love you too," she said, turning to face me. "What's gotten into you?" Caroline's face lit up inquisitively as she readjusted the bold, black-framed Moncler sunglasses on her face.

"It's just really nice to have that chapter officially closed." We sat down at an open bistro table as I continued. "Sophie was nowhere to be found but left Jen a note that she had left for London."

Caroline shrugged. "Of course, that's typical Sophie. Never wants to take responsibility for anything." Her red-golden hair glowed in the sun, fluffy from the recent wash.

God her hair is amazing.

The waiter came by and poured us each a glass of water, handing us the menus. We held the comfortable silence for a moment as we looked it over. Putting down the list of options, I watched as the locals hurried by, picking out tourists easily. The waiter came by and we gave our brief order. It wasn't long before he came back with a bottle and poured us each a generous glass.

"Cheers," I said, raising my glass. "Here's to an official closing of one chapter and the start of a new book."

"Cheers." We clinked glasses as she leaned in to kiss me. "Thank you."

Confused, I asked, "What for? Jen was my problem. Very much my problem."

Caroline shook her head. "Not for that. Don't get me wrong, I am grateful that issue is resolved. I mean, thank you for being—" She paused. "—my person." She nodded and I wasn't sure if she was trying to convince herself or me.

The corners of my mouth lifted. "Your person?" I leaned into the conversation, almost expecting a secret.

Caroline reciprocated, leaning a little over the table. "Yeah." She nodded, more reassured this time. "The person I can count on, the person I can trust with everything, the person I can be with one-hundred percent of the time and love every minute of it."

I took her hand in mine. "To be honest, I never feel like I'm good enough for you."

She made a little pout. "How's that?"

"You've accomplished so much. You follow your dreams. You have crossed so many hurdles in getting here. I don't think I could ever do that."

Caroline brushed it off with the wave of her hand. "Please, you and I had very different paths. I got lucky. It helps when your father owns a Hollywood production company. After he passed, I was simply determined to keep on the path he had catapulted me down. Being born into luck is different than making your own." She took a sip. "You actually had to work for everything. From scratch no less."

Caroline barely ever mentioned her family, especially her father. He had died many years ago and there was always a twang of melancholy when she spoke about him. She had definitely been Daddy's little girl.

I shrugged. "There aren't too many designers that make it, especially ones that get recruited into a major fashion house five years after their first show."

"My love." Caroline put her hand on mine. "Give yourself more credit. I asked you to be on my team because you turned that wreck of Georgi's line into a phenomenal success. Do you remember just how awful that was? That line sold out thanks to you."

With only two years of fashion marketing experience under my belt, I had relied on my financial background to carry me through and make sense of the chaos that was Georgi's line.

I nodded. "I know. We actually oversold certain pieces."

"Exactly. The whole line was an appalling contribution to the world of fashion." She smirked. "Do you remember that yellow and orange peacock accent dress with lime green crinoline? That thing should have been torched but somehow you managed to package that as a hundred-thousand-dollar dress, and it went the day of the exhibition show." She paused. "Frankly, you're my safety net. I asked for Francesco to hire you because even if I fail as a designer, I know you have my back."

"And front." I smirked.

She rolled her eyes. "Yeah, yeah, that too. Seriously though, I really appreciate you wanting to do this with me."

I smiled, knowing I had made a calculated and rational decision in coming over. Although Caroline was unlikely to fail, if she did, I knew how to save the season. I was a quick study when it came to reading people and creating a base of clientele that would be responsive to any fashion creation. And if she was an overwhelming success like I believed, I would come out as the production spine who orchestrated the whole affair. As cold as my calculation may have been, I wasn't willing to risk years of hard work on the whims of the heart.

We finished the plate of olives and cured meats over lighthearted chatter. By now, Caroline and I could finish a bottle of wine with ease at lunch. House wine was much lighter than the full-bodies I was so used to ordering.

I leaned back in my chair, swirling the last few drops in my glass. "Babe? Do you want to take a walk back to the apartment?"

She raised an eyebrow. "To do?"

"I could suggest we play a board game but, if you're into it, I have a different game in mind." I let my demeanor be as flirtatious and as provoking as possible. "A much dirtier game."

Caroline leaned in a little. "Really? Why now? You haven't wanted to try anything lately."

"I think this whole thing with Jen has made me realize just how well you and I fit together."

"Do you trust me?" Caroline asked, fiddling with her glass.

"I trust you."

"A hundred percent?"

I sighed a little, making sure my voice was still

upbeat. "Working on it. Baby steps, babe."

I don't think I can trust anyone fully. I don't know if that's feasible for me anymore. But I trust her more than anyone else.

****

"Be right back." Caroline excused herself to the bathroom as we walked into our apartment.

I knew I had a few minutes to get ready. I searched through the closet for my black corset with viper waist, pulling out a pair of black fishnets and garter to match. I found my tallest slip on black platforms and threw on the outfit. Corset tight around my waist, I stepped out to the dining room to find some scented candles. I lined the windows with them, lighting up the scents of vanilla and jasmine. I pulled the blinds down a little and dimmed the lights. The atmosphere was a good balance between love and desire.

"Babe," I called out, "don't come out of there with anything but your bra and panties, okay?"

I could hear her giggle. "Sure."

Too cute.

The air filled with the scent of the candles. I pulled out the black ropes and dog collar, setting them on the table with my jewel encrusted whip. I admired the collar. It too had little rhinestones throughout. I heard the door creak a little as Caroline emerged.

Even though she was a few years older than I, her body was well toned and lean. Her ab muscles were outlined by the flickers of the candles. Caroline's rose-blonde hair flowed around her shoulders, forming a golden curtain. She was wearing a white lace bra, unlined, letting her nipples tease me, erect under the fabric. Her thong matched, adorned with two little ribbon bows on the sides.

I am so lucky.

I couldn't help but smile at her beauty as I motioned for her to come forward. I took her face between my palms and planted a loving kiss on her rouged lips. "I love you. We're going to take this at our own pace. We need to learn what we each like and what our boundaries are. The only expectation I have of you is to communicate to me. Will that work for you?"

Caroline looked at me from under her long lashes. "I love you too and yes, that's a deal."

"Final question," I asked, stroking her hair back. "Do you want us to have a safety word?"

Shrugging she replied, "I don't think we need one. You know me."

I nodded, reverting myself into a version of Mistress. "Kneel, my little one," I told her, taking the collar off the counter. I moved her luscious hair to one side, exposing her neck. I looked at her, bowing her head submissively, and I found myself conflicted.

"Little one" is more endearing than "pet."

I placed the collar gently around her neck, fastening the buckle securely but generously around her. I couldn't help but kiss the top of her head. With Jen I never had any hesitations. Despite Caroline's willingness, I found myself taking my time as I placed a blindfold around her eyes.

I led her to stand. "You good?" She nodded in reply. I took the tip of the whip and ran it over her shoulders, down her spine. Caroline shivered and started to breathe through her mouth. I grazed my nails over her tender skin, wanting to remember every line, every freckle, and every little nuance.

Can I truly trust her? Can I really let my guard down?

I stood behind her, watching the rise and fall of her shoulders, and pulled her hands back behind her, holding her wrists together. Pressing my body against hers, I ran my fingers over her breasts, taking the time to playfully pinch her nipples. I kissed her neck longingly.

I have her, I love her, but somehow, I want more of her.

I bit her shoulder gently as I let my hand brush over her stomach. She squirmed against me. "That tickles," she whispered.

"Shush, my little one." I smiled in reply. I placed my hands on either side of her hips and turned her toward the kitchen counter. Placing both of her palms on the counter edge, I pulled her hips toward me, forcing her to bend over farther. I kissed her shoulder blades as I ran my hands down the front of her body. Stepping to the side, I ran the whip over her again, this time slapping her lightly with it as I passed over her ass. She jerked slightly, a little surprised. "Breathe, my love," I whispered. I saw her spine relax as she exhaled, and I tapped her again. She didn't flinch. Taking the whip end between her legs, I teased her clit with a gentle rub of the leather tip. I ran the whip up and down her inner thighs. Caroline breathed a little heavier as I teased the outside of her thong.

"I want more," she murmured. Her hands gripped the edge of the granite stone.

I responded with a faintly harder slap of my hand on her ass. I repeated until she let out a little moan.

"My little one, lean so your back is straight," I

commanded. Caroline complied as I placed the whip handle between her shoulder blades, letting the shaft run along her spine, tucking the tip into the top of her thong's waistband. "Don't move," I whispered in her ear. "And don't let it fall." I watched her face for a reaction. Her mouth was parted slightly as she grinned to one side.

"Yes, Mistress."

Mistress sounds so cold. I should think about changing that. Or should I? Why am I finding this such a challenge? I feel like this is my first time.

I stood behind her and ran my hands down her stomach, teasing the top of her pelvis. She squirmed but remained still after the whip rolled a little between her shoulders. I pushed my fingers between her and the fabric, feeling Caroline already drenched with excitement.

"Someone enjoys this," I softly exclaimed.

If she's this wet, she must like it. Her body wouldn't lie.

I found her clit and began to tease her with my fingertips. Caroline gripped the counter harder as I circled a little more intensely. I let my fingers dance around her, only hinting at what was to come. Her wetness completely covering my fingers, I entered her with one, curling it to play with her G-spot. Caroline dropped her head, trying hard not to move her back. She let out a groan. I entered her with two fingers, and she couldn't keep it together anymore. The whip fell to the ground. Caroline froze. Guilt flashed over her face as she removed her blindfold.

"Oh, my little one, you have much to learn. Go on your knees, pick it up, and present it to me." Caroline followed the instructions, presenting the whip to me, casting her eyes down. "You also removed your blindfold. What do you have to say for yourself?"

She's adorable. How could I ever be a mean Mistress to her?

Caroline's nose flared. "I'm sorry…" She looked up at me with a concerned playfulness.

"Are you?" I tried to make my voice seem stern, but I couldn't help but grin.

She maintained eye contact. "Yes."

I ran the whip over her shoulder, gently caressing her. "Yes, what?"

Caroline lowered her eyes. "Yes, Mistress."

Okay, maybe Mistress still works. Oh Caroline, you're just too…you, and I love every ounce of you.

Maintaining my composure as a seemingly gentle Mistress, I continued, "Very well. Remove your thong, perch yourself up on the counter, and put your blindfold back on." As Caroline executed her commands, I unwound the rope, pulling two heavy stools on either side of her. I placed her bare feet on each seat and tied them loosely to the stool backs. I pushed the stools out a little, forcing her to spread wider. "These are quick release knots so if you decide you've had enough, just say the word."

"Yes, Mistress."

Caroline leaned back on her palms. I pushed her chest down with the whip end. "On your forearms and move your bum to the edge of the counter." I adjusted the stools again. I played with her once again with my fingers. Pressing lightly on her clit, letting the tension rebuild. I slid a couple fingers inside of her and she inhaled sharply. I kept steady. "Do you think I should let you cum since you failed at your simple task?"

Caroline took a second to reply. "Whatever Mistress thinks I deserve." Her voice raised as if questioning her own response.

You deserve everything you want. I will give you anything you want.

I folded my hand narrowly and almost managed my three knuckles into her. I saw her chest rise and fall rapidly. "Shush, little one, relax and accept. One day you will want to do this to yourself and let me do you from behind with a strap on." Her muscles contracted around my fingers at the thought, and I felt her squirt just a little. I looked at her, her blindfolded face seemingly pleased at the thought.

I bent over, kissing her, fingers still inside of her, playing gently. Caroline relaxed and let her head drop behind her. I started to lick her, teasing with the tip of my tongue. Caroline moaned as she exhaled. She reached for my head.

"Don't touch."

Even though I want you to touch. I want your hands on me. In me. Anywhere.

She retracted her hand quickly and I sucked on her a little harder. I pushed my fingers in deeper, using my thumb to add additional pressure to her clit. Caroline's hands clenched over the surface of the counter, not knowing what to grab. My other hand ran the length of her inner thigh, keeping her spread widely against the stools. Her feet struggled against the ties. As her breathing rate increased, I knew she was close. I reached for her hand and she gripped it tightly. Caroline let her head fall, arching her back. Her hold became clenching as she let out an exasperated cry. I pressed my tongue a touch harder and Caroline let out another moan, swearing in the process. Her body accepted the rush of pleasure and I did my best to let the feeling linger. She released the grip on my hand and lay flat on the counter, breathing heavily. I released the knots and walked around to kiss her lips upside-down.

I whispered into her ear, "You're lucky Mistress loves you." I removed her blindfold gently, letting her brilliant-green, contented eyes look up at me.

"I am lucky." She smiled contentedly.

You deserve all the pleasure I can provide you.

I kissed her again deeply. Caroline propped herself up on the counter, taking a single stride back down to the floor. She held onto the counter ledge, not trusting her legs yet. I met her on the other side of the counter again, pushing the small of her back against the marble edge, holding her close to me once more.

I felt Caroline's breath against my ear as she whispered, "What about you?"

"We can take care of me after dinner," I offered. It didn't matter to me. I only wanted to make her happy, and I knew it would be an exercise in futility if she tried to get me off. I was easy to please but the hardest to make cum.

She walked to the bathroom clutching her thong. "I don't even know…" Her voice trailed off as she closed the bathroom door.

I heard an exasperated, "Holy crap" from within the bathroom.

"What's wrong?" I trotted over to the door. "Everything okay?"

She opened the door slightly and I could see that she had removed her bra already. Caroline's smile was wide as she exclaimed, "I can't wear these anymore! They're drenched." She paused, looking back toward the door. "I actually need to shower. What did you do to me?" She was laughing now. "Hey, love?"

I pushed open the door. "Yes, babe?"

"Thank you for indulging my curiosity." She blew me an air kiss as she opened the door and stepped into the glass shower.

I will do anything for you.

Chapter Fourteen

The spring collection was well underway, the sun gleaming outside the windows of Caroline's studio as she was making her first samples on the measuring bust. We had been in Milan for almost a year now and we were both content with our new home. Caroline's line had been growing in popularity, opening for another Valentino show as well as having a couple small shows on her own. We had stayed best friends and respected co-workers, despite adding the romantic relationship into the mix. It was a comfortable place for the both of us and Caroline seemed happy. For the first time in a long time, I was happy.

I sipped on my coffee as I let my thoughts wander. Not wanting to work on the promo marketing dynamics yet for the collection, I stared out the window watching the Vespas speed by. I counted all the red ones, a childhood habit. I counted five before a black car pulled up in front of the building door. Francesco stepped out followed by a lady wearing an exaggerated black hat. I looked over at Caroline kneeling in front of a sizing manikin. "Babe, are we expecting someone this morning? I didn't think there were any fit models or assistants coming in today."

Caroline looked at me with tailoring pins in hand. "Not that I know of. Francesco said he might drop by but that was about it."

I heard the footsteps on the stairs getting louder. There was a knock on the open door as Francesco let himself in.

"Ladies, we have a visitor," he exclaimed. "A visitor who needs something custom." His eyebrows lifted, adding intrigue to his announcement.

Caroline stood as he entered farther into the room. The brim of the black hat appeared around the corner, covering a slender woman's face. I stayed by the window, leaning against its frame.

Francesco proudly announced to us, "Let me introduce you both to Miss Alessandra."

"Of course, Miss Alessandra." She stuck out her hand to the guest. "I'm Caroline. It's a pleasure to meet you."

Dark eyes and fiery red lipstick were unleashed from under the hat. "*Ciao*, the pleasure is mine." Her voice was stern and very unwelcoming.

Caroline looked back at me and I joined the two ladies in the exchange of greetings. Her handshake was soft, but her eyes stayed like daggers, piercing the soul.

Jeez, I wouldn't want to get on your bad side.

Her mouth moved only to speak, showing no emotion whatsoever. Alessandra removed her coat and hat, passing them to an eagerly awaiting Francesco. Now I could see her for who she was, and it dawned on me as to why Francesco was so doting.

This 'Miss Alessandra' was a very popular, local celebrity on the small screen, making a recent debut in a Hollywood production set for global release shortly. I had seen her photos all over pop-culture websites and on several billboards around town.

There was an awkward pause until Francesco piped

up, "We need to make a gown for Miss Alessandra's red carpet premier next month."

I could feel Caroline already start to panic a bit.

"We also need to finish the deadline for the winter line," Caroline immediately protested.

Oh, my lovely Carol, it'll be just fine.

Francesco waved a hand in the air. "*Carissima*, you have worked miracles, you will do it again."

Caroline sighed. "What are you hoping for, Miss Alessandra? A 'wow' factor, something elegant but daring, or something downright different?"

"I want myself as a gown," she said barely moving a muscle, looking rather bored already. "You need to impress me. Francesco has already assured me that I won't be disappointed." She continued to add onto the mounting pressure. "I expect to be more than satisfied by your design." Another uncomfortable pause lingered in the room.

"You would like me to embody you as a piece of clothing," Caroline clarified. "Any color tones that you…"

She waived a hand in the air. "Precisely," she said, cutting Caroline off and snapping her fingers for her coat again. "I'll await your call for a fitting. Francesco has my details."

I couldn't help my reaction. I was intrigued. My impulsive Mistress side immediately wanted to know what it would be like to have her as a pet.

Perhaps 'bitchy' is a good look on you, Miss Alessandra. I could show you how to be submissive. I don't like you, but I wouldn't mind the challenge of doing you.

Caroline held her composure well despite the

frostbitten mannerism. "You're a thirty-six, twenty-six, thirty-eight and a shoe size…" Caroline glanced down. "Thirty-seven, and you're just under five foot seven. Is that correct?"

Alessandra looked over the brim of her glasses. "Hmm-hmm." With that, she left abruptly, leaving a moderately frantic Francesco in her wake. He dashed after her but not before making an eye-roll in our direction. Caroline managed a smiled and waved him out of the studio. I went back to my spot by the window to watch them leave.

I want to dominate you, Miss Alessandra.

Caroline's voice immediately made me flash back into reality. "I'm going for a puff. Coming?"

I'm with Caroline. I can't think these thoughts.

I trailed Caroline down the stairs and stepped out into the sunshine.

Threesome?

"Did you know?" Caroline seemed a little more goaded now.

I shrugged. "Well, like you, I had heard rumors but nothing concrete. Can't say I'm surprised. It's about time Francesco got you a celebrity sponsor."

"She seems…" Caroline let out a long exhale. "Like a bit of a challenge."

A challenge I wouldn't mind tying down to the bed and teasing until she begged me to let her cum.

I adjusted my foot against the wall, leaning my back against the warmed concrete. I kept my voice steady as I replied, "Nothing you're not used to by now. Just look at me. I'm no walk in the park." I closed my eyes enjoying the sun's warmth.

I would make her work for it. I want to do her from

behind with a strap on...maybe a double. Contain yourself!

Caroline chuckled a little. "But I love you, I'm not in love with her." Caroline held her gaze at me. "You found her interesting, didn't you?"

I smiled a little. "You didn't?" I kept my eyes closed, letting Caroline judge my demeanor.

Threesome? Maybe?

"Sure, in that bitchy, dark, mysterious way, she may be entertaining." Caroline pondered for a moment longer.

Her head pressing into me as she ate me out. I want those dark, commanding eyes to become subservient.

I shook my head, trying to force the dirty thoughts out of my mind and instead focused on the feeling of sun on my face. I smelled the smoke of Caroline's vape flow over my face as she exhaled.

She cleared her throat. "I was thinking about this last night and I don't think I have ever asked you—do you ever miss being with guys?"

I looked at her out of the corner of my eye, questioning the sudden inquiry. I shrugged. "They have their merits, I suppose, but adding love and trust into the mix is where it gets complicated for me. I've asked myself so many times, but I think it comes down to feeling less threatened with a girl. But I do battle whether or not I was ever actually attracted to men. Sometimes I think it was just a result of how I was brought up."

Caroline nodded, almost understanding, but then asked, "Physically or emotionally?"

"Threatened? Physically not with girls. I like mine

petite." I winked at her. "But emotionally? I have worried in the past about some issues. Girls tend to get overly jealous. Case and point with Jen, but if you can find the right person, it tends to work out—like with us. So much of it is trust for me."

Caroline joined me, leaning against the wall with her shoulder. She lowered her voice a little. "Do you think that's what led you to like the Dominant thing?"

I couldn't help but smile as I reflected.

Oh Carol, you're too sweet. There's so much more to...all of this. I don't even understand why Mistress is appealing sometimes. I want you and love you, but I want to dominate that bitchy, mysterious girl.

I collected myself quickly. "You know how we can either do Vanilla or go Cookies and Cream, and for us, both are amazing? I don't mind doing the Dominant thing, but if we didn't have the regular, there wouldn't be a connection for me to trust and work from." A puff of cherry blew past my nostrils and I indulged in the sweet smell. "I will say though, that I can't be submissive, that doesn't work out for me well."

"What happens?" There was a trace of concern in her voice but primarily her tone was filled with curiosity.

I turned to face her. "Well..." I shrugged. "Last time it was with a guy and we weren't even doing anything crazy, but he held me down, and I guess since I hadn't formed that bond of trust with him, I had a panic attack right in the middle of everything."

I hated it. Absolutely hated it.

Caroline let out a giggle. "Sorry, but that would be pretty humorous...you know, after the fact."

I rolled my eyes at her. "At the time I think it

freaked me out more than anything, but I haven't put myself into that position since then. Freaked the hell out of him too." I managed to let out a forced chuckle.

"You let me hold you down sometimes," she said cautiously.

"Babe, I love you and you weigh, what, a hundred pounds? You're tiny. I can flip you and pin you in an instant." I leaned closer into her, taking a lock of her hair between my fingers. "And you know I will just for fun." I kissed her at the tail end of an exhale, sparking a teasing tongue touch. My lips lingered on hers.

I love kissing her.

The moment was rudely interrupted as Caroline's phone buzzed from her pocket—it was Francesco. She paced a little as they talked, hanging up shortly after.

She came back over with a rather gloomy look on her face. "He wants us to entertain Alessandra tonight in order to get to know what she's like. Well, me specifically, but I'm roping you into it too. He says she's staying at the Mandarin Oriental."

Just how well do we want to get to know her? I wouldn't mind watching a pet Alessandra and my beautiful girl go at it together.

I brought Caroline closer to me, draping my arm over her shoulders. "That's perfectly fine. Not an issue. Let's go to that new joint that opened on the boulevard. I know the owner. It's all the rage these days. We can hit up a lounge bar after."

"Can you..." Caroline wasn't a fan of arranging details. She was organized in so many ways, but scheduling was definitely not one of them.

"Already on it." I sent a quick message to the owner, who replied seconds later. "Marco says he'll have a table ready at nine-thirty tonight. I'll send a car for her." Caroline kissed my cheek and we headed back upstairs.

The rest of the afternoon was fairly quiet with Caroline humming and hawing about her choice of finishes. I busied myself in the spring line's advertising strategy, trying to ignore the ravenous thoughts about Alessandra that kept creeping into my head. I had a lot of work on my plate. This show would be Caroline's first dedicated show and it had to be perfect. Having already solidified the venue almost a year ago in Paris, now all that was left was the execution of a seemingly never-ending list of details. The show marked the launch of her brand being showcased within the Parisian lineup of Fashion Week. It was the next step to becoming an international sensation. Bella Vita's editor had remained fairly quiet after Caroline's introduction into the fashion world as a solo artist, but her assistant had RSVP'd within minutes of receiving this show's invitation.

She would look amazing in a dog collar, spiky heels, and nipple clamps...kneeling between Caroline's legs, eating her out...

I shook my head and refocused on the supplies list I was creating.

A large anal plug...maybe one with a jewel or maybe rabbit...focus.

I re-read the list twice to make sure I hadn't accidentally added "large anal toy" to the list and attached it to an email to the team's coordinating assistant, Gina.

I'd love to tie Caroline up to the headboard...with Alessandra licking and nibbling on her nipples...I can eat her out…both of them out…Dear lord, keep it together.

I desperately tried to refocus by finishing my email. I asked Gina to schedule time with the fabric manufacturer tomorrow. Regardless if I hated or loved going to find fabric, Caroline would want fresh spools to use for Alessandra's gown that hadn't hit the mainstream market yet.

Take her on the counter, spread her legs…taste her…

Coming out of my daze, I picked up my ringing phone. "*Pronto?*"

"*Ciao.* It's Gina. I wanted to ask if you were sure about going to the fabric people tomorrow." Her voice was squeaky on the phone as she did her best to process her sentence in broken English.

I answered the retort as pleasantly as possible. "Yes, I'm sure. We have a new project."

"I don't see any on the list," she protested. Gina was not a fan of doing tasks in a rushed manner or doing anything for that matter.

"Gina, please just arrange it for tomorrow." I shook my head to myself as I got up from the desk.

The protesting continued. "But Carol was just there."

"Gina, why is this an issue? Arrange it for tomorrow, please. We need exclusivity of the facility. No prying eyes like last time." My tone had gradually gone from pleasant to highly annoyed. Caroline looked over at me with an eyebrow raised.

"I think they're closed tomorrow. I don't think they will—"

"Gina, we spent over half a million Euros there last

year. Figure it out." I hung up abruptly.

Caroline put her feet up on her foot stool, taking out her sketchbook. "She irritates me too. When I ask her for something basic it always seems to be such an issue."

I rolled my eyes. "If she weren't Francesco's cousin, she wouldn't have a job. Anyway, if she manages to do what I asked, we will have an appointment over at your favorite fabric place." The name eluded me. "That one by the museum."

She looked up from her page. "How'd you know I wanted to go there?"

"Babe, I know you. You always like starting with a fresh page when it comes to your designs, and that also means fabric." I sat back down at my desk, opening the revised fabric budget for Miss Alessandra to see how much room we had for this gown.

She blew me an air kiss. "I love you."

"Love you too," I said, returning the kiss. Residual thoughts about Alessandra floated away into the not-so-far distance as I scrolled through my historical fabric invoices, looking for the collective amount we had spent at this fabric place last year.

Caroline's voice interrupted my attempt at distraction. "Hun, do you ever think about future us?"

"Future us as in marriage and kids and all that jazz?" I looked over at her. She was still sketching.

Marriage. Really, are we having this conversation already? Threesome to kids? No. No thanks. I guess she wasn't really a part of the threesome discussion between me, myself, and I but...maybe I could ask? Holy moly, just stop.

I shook my head at myself.

She nodded briefly. "Of course, but I'm not sure if you would want that." She put down her sketch pen and came over to sit on my desk.

You're right, I don't want all of that.

"You've come so far already," I stated, taking a strand of her hair between my fingers. "I didn't know if you would want all of that either."

"I've come a long way?"

Far enough for a threesome? I can hope I suppose.

I nodded. "Babe, I've known you for years. When I first met you, you were with Sophie and you tried to make things work. She broke your heart and you put up barriers that were sky high. Then you went through a number of girls because that's what suited you, and you know I say that holding no judgement, simply stating the facts." Caroline looked at me in silence, but her demeanor was shy. "I'm proud of you, but even more thankful to you for letting me in and letting your guard down. You are the love of my life. You are my best friend, and I can't imagine being with anyone else. I want to make you happy."

I guess I can think about this marriage thing. I can't string her along like I did with Jen. And Caroline is most definitely not Jen. Kids though—hell no.

Caroline pulled my wheeled chair in front of her, putting her feet up on either side of my hips. "You do make me happy. You make me happier than anyone I have been with romantically or as a friend. I'm scared that after what happened with Jen, settling down would be out of the question."

I'm a little scared too.

I stared through her for a second.

Can I honestly one-hundred percent trust

Caroline? Maybe? She's never given me a reason to disbelieve. Do I have to worry about my own thoughts or fantasies? Only if I were to act on them, right?

I returned the ball into her court. "How do you envision settling down? Is it doing what you love for work? Traveling the world, showcasing your designs and exploring new places?"

She shrugged. "I want all of that. At my age though kids aren't really something I'm entertaining."

Thank God.

Caroline continued. "But maybe you still like real dicks too and having kids is something that you can do, or I guess, adopt, or whatever...but I really just don't want any right now and it won't be coming up in the future." Caroline's gaze didn't know where to settle after her blundering statement. "Are you okay with that?" she added quickly.

I smiled. "You're only a little older than me, silly. Regardless, I would rather travel the world, spend my life with you, and continue to be us rather than have children. So yes, I'm okay with that."

"Even though society..."

"The hell with society's expectations. Babe, we're going to have a life adventure on our own and that works for me."

Caroline brought me between her legs. "I understand if you need that part of life to be fulfilled. I thought I did at one point too." Caroline paused. "What about your parents?" Caroline raised an eyebrow, knowing I barely ever talked to them anymore.

I took her hand in mine. "My mother doesn't even know I'm bi."

Bisexual? Pansexual? Lesbian? Does the label

161

matter?

Caroline looked at me surprised. "She doesn't? How?"

I shrugged. "She professed a very high disdain for lesbianism when I was young and confused. I remember the day I asked her if I was straight or not, and she told me that I was questioning my sexual preferences because my boyfriend wasn't very good looking." I paused, recalling the moment like it had just happened. I continued as neutrally as possible. "She said I wouldn't think twice about it if I was dating someone who was as good looking as Clooney or a physically fit DiCaprio." Alleviating the tension, I half laughed at the memory. "Babe, you know I was brought up to be a 'proper young woman' by someone who has a Catholic background and whose own mother was raised by nuns. My mother always did her best for me, but trust me when I say bisexuality most definitely does not fit within her definition of 'proper.' She will be disappointed about the lack of grandkids, I'm sure, but her rage for me being in a lifetime relationship with a girl, regardless of who, is something she will not be able to comprehend."

Caroline took a deep breath. "That's a lot to process." She thought a moment longer. "And what about your dad?"

I sighed. "My father supports me when it's convenient for him or when he knows it'll piss off my mother. I doubt he will have much of an opinion about kids." I waved my hand dismissively. "He'll be half disgusted, and half intrigued by our relationship. He and I are very, shall we say, cordial with one another but nothing much of the heart passes between us."

She shook her head. "From what you've shared with me over the years, I don't know how they managed to stay together. Regardless, though, I have a request." Caroline became serious in her tone.

"Shoot." I took her hands in mine.

"I need you to be open to your parents about us."

Could have seen that one coming.

I looked into her eyes. "I promise I will introduce you and be transparent with them." I kissed the top of her hand. "I will need to buy you a bulletproof vest beforehand, but it'll happen."

It'll be like going through a war zone.

I smirked a little. "No joke about the vest." Trying to deflect any more questions, I asked, "What about your mom?"

Caroline rolled her eyes. "What about her?"

"Does she know?"

Caroline slapped my shoulder. "Of course she knows, silly. I've always been lesbian. No two ways about it. Kissed my first girl at age six. Poor blondie didn't know what hit her." Caroline let out a hearty laugh. "Mom had a serious chat with me that night. It didn't faze my dad at all. He probably thought it would make a good episode on one of his shows."

I couldn't help but let out a little chuckle. "What about the kids thing?"

"Oh please! My mom is off gallivanting around on her yacht somewhere with a boatload of twenty-something, eight-pack abs with Australian accents. Angela couldn't care less. Being responsible has never been her thing. On the contrary, being wealthy and irresponsible suits her just fine, but having grandkids would just cramp her style." We stayed silent for a minute, staring at each other. I stood between her legs and wrapped my arms around her. Caroline hugged my waist, intertwining her fingers behind my back.

No kids. I can think about the marriage thing. I could do this. It wouldn't be that hard. Sure. I can do this.

"Just us two," I whispered.

"Just us two," she echoed.

Occasional three? Guilty as charged—I want a side of extra sprinkles on my ice cream.

Chapter Fifteen

We were meeting Alessandra in less than an hour and Caroline was having a 'nothing to wear' moment. I called out to her, "Babe, what about the dress that you wore to the Versace show? It's not too much for tonight but still has a ton of flare." I stood in the doorway of the walk-through closet fully dressed and ready to go.

Caroline peeked around the corner of the bathroom holding a mascara wand. "Don't you think there will be paparazzi? I should wear something I already wore?"

"Different accessories change the look." I shrugged. "You did all black last time. Why don't you try it with a metallic or a pop of red or something brighter?"

"Can you find those silvery Louboutin stilettos? They should be on the rack."

There was one thing that every fashion industry couple, especially two very feminine women, needed— a massive closet. Upon picking this apartment we had decided to take the second bedroom and make it into a closet, connecting to the master en suite. It was a large, generous space but still not large enough. In true fashion to both our tastes, we had installed a floor to ceiling shoe and handbag display. The closet was mainly filled with Caroline's things, but we did share a few things here and there including footwear. At only half a shoe size difference we made things work, and clothes were basically interchangeable. I grabbed her silver shoes and a newer designer purse with metallic details, and a flash of their house green and red ribbon. I pulled the black dress off the rack. The light, airy fabric of the dress shimmered a little with residual glitter from the prior wear.

"Will this work?" I presented the outfit to her. "Maybe with your motto jacket?"

Caroline smiled. "This is why I love you." She kissed me on the cheek and took the dress from me, unzipping the back zip. "You always know what I want to wear even when I don't."

I looked at the clock on the bedside table. We were going to be late. "Ironic since you make a lot of what's in this closet. I have to call Sebastian, otherwise we will be more than fashionably late. Will you be okay to leave in five?" I got a thumbs up from the bathroom door paired with a muffled 'Yes,' and I texted for our driver to meet us downstairs.

****

By the time Alessandra showed up, Caroline and I were already a drink in, working on our seconds. Like any popular celebrity, she entered by the back of the restaurant to avoid whatever crowd was outside. Marco had designated us the corner of his restaurant and hired additional security for the night. He was thrilled to have a local celebrity guest and had already told me he was covering the evening's expenses as a demonstration of his gratitude.

Alessandra arrived in a deep purple trumpet dress, ending right above the knee. Its plunging neckline left little to the imagination whilst her dangling pendant necklace only teased for more attention. It was a mix of classic Italian flair and Bella Vita in the eighties.

She cleans up well. Look at those firm breasts. Look at those curves. Shut up.

We stood to greet her, giving a cordial peck on each cheek. She was almost as frigid as earlier, seemingly forcing the reciprocation. I looked at Caroline who returned my questioning stare with a small shrug of the shoulders.

Caroline was sandwiched between us in the semi-circle booth. I could tell she was a little uncomfortable making small talk, struggling to get Alessandra to reply with more than a couple of words.

Having been forewarned by Francesco as to her likes and dislikes, I had pre-ordered a bottle of champagne and a bottle of red in addition to selecting menu items. Marco had assigned two dedicated staff members to the table, so beverage and food were quickly served. Alessandra finished a glass of champagne within minutes of receiving it and was well into her second. Her words became a little more flowing, but she seemed preoccupied, nonetheless. It was a loud restaurant, proving it difficult to have conversation across the table, but Caroline was really doing her best. As Alessandra stood for the bathroom, two bodyguards appeared in tow as she walked briskly away.

Caroline grabbed my knee with urgency. "Holy shit, it's like talking to a wall. When she does speak, it's so fast it's like a squirrel with a heavy accent. Blah. Can you please switch with me? Please?"

I laughed. "Don't you need to learn about her to get the perfect 'Miss Alessandra dress'?"

She rolled her eyes dramatically. "I know her top

color choices and cuts she prefers. That's all I could drag out of her. Please, you're good at extracting information. Just switch with me. I'm going to go outside for a sec once she gets back. I need a breather."

"I don't know if I'll get anywhere but sure, I can try." It was true—one of my strengths was getting people to open up to me. Alessandra returned and Caroline excused herself promptly to the ladies as well.

Her perfume filled the air beside me. "I see you have been left to deal with the *Dramatic Italian*," she said, mocking herself. "I think I make your designer friend feel uncomfortable." She grabbed a fresh glass of champagne off the table.

You have a sense of humor?

I tried not to let my puzzled thoughts show. "Caroline is flattered you chose her to make a dress for you. She just wants to make sure she gets it right."

I watched as her eyes scanned the room, ignoring anyone who met her gaze.

Those eyes, what would it be like if they stared up at me whilst sucking between my legs?

"I'm sure that's all it is." She smirked. Her eyes were rimmed by black, shimmery eyeliner outlining a full set of eyelashes.

You would be such a challenge. I want to try. Stop. Seriously.

I collected myself again. "So, Miss Alessandra—"

"Please." She waved. "Just Alessandra, even Allie is fine. That's what my friends call me. Believe me, I'm not that stuck up." She crossed her legs, shifting toward me, taking her third glass of champagne.

Look at those legs. Those thighs are perfect. I could spread those thighs. Shut up. Focus. Work.

I smiled at her, trying to turn my libido off. Taking my glass from the table I asked, "Allie, what do you do when you're not on set?"

She sighed with melancholy. "I used to dance. Everything from ballet to tap, but my favorite was always the tango."

Dear lord, this just gets harder and harder. I can only imagine how your body moves.

I kept my voice calm, my fingers dancing with the glass as a form of distraction. "You don't anymore?"

She shrugged. "My agent says that talent won't get me far in my work. I danced for over ten years but now I only do it for fun, when I can find the time."

I looked at her inquisitively. "Why the tango?"

"The passion," she answered. "I am a shy person and I don't like talking. Believe it or not, I don't like being the center of attention. But tango dancing lets me embrace my own person, show the anger, pain, or love I have in my heart. I don't have to say anything, yet the dance tells everyone what I want to say."

I looked at her, perplexed by her gloomy, tough exterior and seemingly soft interior. "That must be why you enjoy acting?"

Her eyelashes fluttered. "You assume I enjoy it? Acting is what worked, it's not my first choice of career. I blame an over eager mother. The industry is…too much…" She made circles in the air with her hands. "But I do try and enjoy it. When my agent finds a good role, one that I can really relate to, it works best."

"Your mom must be proud of you," I offered.

Allie took a long sip of champagne, finishing her glass. "My mother will never be very proud. She always wants me to do more."

I dismissed the comment with a slight hand wave. "Doesn't matter. The only person who needs to be proud is you, and you should be proud. You've come this far, and you don't even have the passion of love behind it."

The comment earned me a smile from her dark ruby lips. Caroline rejoined the table, raising her eyebrow at me. I returned it with a reassuring nod. With Allie's guard farther down and four glasses of champagne in, the conversation was a little more flowing at the table. Marco came by to say hello and extend his gratitude for Allie's visit. Even though our conversation was brief, I could tell she was pretending not to be mortified.

I want to take her to bed. Work. Okay. What do I do? I need to get her to be her. Dance.

I leaned over to Caroline as the food was being taken away. "I have an idea, but I need you to roll with it."

Caroline nodded, confused. "Sure, what are you thinking?"

"You'll see. I'm going to get Sebastian to pull around back, and I'll meet you out there in a few?" Caroline reluctantly agreed and I stepped outside through the back door of the restaurant. I started searching my contacts list for our next destination. The car pulled up and Sebastian put the car into park, stepping out to come stand beside me.

"Sebastian?"

"*Si, Signorina?*"

I showed him my phone screen. "Could you please take us here?"

He looked at me, confused. "Sure, but I thought we were going to the Niche Club?"

"Change of plans. This will be better. There's water in the back, right?" He nodded as I made a call.

Caroline showed up with a slightly tipsy Allie shortly thereafter with her bodyguards in tow. I handed them both bottles of water. "Drink up, you'll need it." The three of us got into the limo while her entourage followed in their sedan. It was a short drive, thankfully. The car pulled up to the building whose pillars rose proudly from the ground to hold up a heavily decorated roof. As Allie's men helped with the doors as we exited the car, I called for the manager to retrieve us from the front door.

"What is this place?" Caroline asked from behind me as we walked quickly down the hall, our heels clicking on the marble floors.

"I think I know," Allie whispered in awe.

I smiled back at them both. "You do."

The manager opened the heavy double doors. "I'll be right back," she said. "Studio shoes are there by the piano." She flicked on the lights, illuminating a large dance studio with fully mirrored walls. I nodded and mouthed a thank you to her.

"How did you manage this?" Allie beamed at the surprise, already making her way to the shoes hanging off the ballet bar.

I shrugged. "Favors are meant to be asked when they're worth asking for." I took Caroline's hand and squeezed it. She looked at me pleasantly surprised.

Allie was fastening her last shoe as the instructor walked in with two other men.

"You're lucky we had rehearsal tonight." He

smiled at me, coming to give me a kiss on either cheek.

I returned his smile. "Thank you for doing this for us."

He held my shoulders between his firm hands. "Anything for the woman who volunteered her time to sell a record number of off-season dance company tickets. We would have died that season in Toronto without that sell-out season." He turned to face Caroline and Alessandra, greeting them with similar enthusiasm. "And you must be the lovely Miss Alessandra De Luca." He reached to kiss the top of her hand. "Charmed."

Allie blushed. "It's such an honor to meet you." Her smile glowed now. "And please call me Allie." She cast a backward glance at me in awe. He seemingly was used to the adoration that Allie so clearly showcased.

"Although not your speed my dear," he said jokingly to me. "Nor Caroline's." He winked. "I hope these two gentlemen will do." He asked the male dancers to shed their jackets before going to plug in his phone to the sound system. Caroline and I came to join a star-struck Allie with our dance shoes on. Neither Caroline nor I knew how to dance, but it didn't matter. The moment was for Allie and the outcome would benefit Caroline.

"So, Allie, a little bird told me you enjoy the tango? Let's do a warmup and see what you can do!" The instructor took Allie as his partner while Caroline and I were led by the other two dancers. The music started slowly, as they walked us through simple steps. I heard Caroline laughing at her two left feet. Not being any better myself, I floundered my way through as gracefully as I could.

I looked between Caroline and Allie, subconsciously comparing the two. Allie was confident in her strides, but very serious in her demeanor. Caroline was less sure about herself, naturally, but having such a good time making a fool of herself. Caroline's hair flowed like a horse's mane with every step. I caught a glimpse of her smile.

She has such a perfect smile.

The instructor paused the music. "Do you know this?" He directed the question to Allie and played a different, much quicker song. She nodded. Caroline and I went to take a seat on the sidelines with our partners—this was no match for either of us.

Allie glided across the room, seemingly now sober and completely in her element. I recalled what she had said earlier about being able to demonstrate her emotions. I watched intently, trying to decipher the puzzle. The grace of her neck flowed to the tip of her fingers as the instructor led her across the room with ease. The instructor moved on to a new song and Allie's feet picked up the passion of the piece. An intensity of frustration and anger were in her first few steps. The instructor helped her mold that into what seemed like sadness and regret and led her into a sense of calm. The song blended into another and they continued what seemed to be dance therapy. By the end of the third song, Alessandra was smiling again, and seemingly at peace with herself.

Caroline leaned over to me and whispered, "I feel like we just watched the eight phases of anger and resolution."

"Faster than going to the shrink," I jested softly.

"How did you know?"

I half shrugged. "She mentioned it when you went outside for a smoke. Tango was a childhood passion of hers."

Allie was still chatting with the instructor with lightheartedness and hugged him before the three men collectively left.

She came to join us on the bench. Sitting down with the slightest huff, she grabbed her water bottle and took a long drink. "That was amazing. I can't believe that you know him."

"I've heard he's pretty good," I said with slight sarcasm as I removed my shoes. "He taught a friend of mine a few years ago, and I ended up helping out his show. The performing arts don't attract as much of a crowd as they should in Toronto."

Allie snorted. "He was the best in the world five years running before retiring and teaching some of the best teams." She shook her head. "I don't know how you ladies pulled this off but thank you, I really needed that."

"It was all her." Caroline put her hand on my thigh and gave me a smile of gratitude, pushing a strand of hair behind her ear.

That smile. Such a perfect smile.

****

Caroline took off her earrings in front of the bedroom mirror, already in her night slip, nipples cold against the satin. She stared at me in the reflection. Already under the covers, I flipped through my emails, earmarking ones to respond to tomorrow morning.

I saw her staring me down in the mirror. "What?" I asked, finally breaking the silence.

She smiled at me, putting her earrings on the

bedside table, slipping off her night dress, and pulling back her side of the covers. "You are truly a terrible dancer."

I looked over at her. "Thank you," I said sarcastically. I put my phone to charge on the nightstand. "You're fairly terrible yourself." The phone buzzed again but I ignored it. Too much work makes for a dull girlfriend. I turned my attention to the beautiful blonde beside me.

Caroline snuggled up beside my shoulder. "What are we going to do if we ever have to dance in public?"

I raised an eyebrow. "What would possess us to do that?"

She hid her face a little, becoming shy in her response. "I don't know," she mumbled.

I scooted down to meet her, kissing her on the nose. "If we are ever dancing in public, we will be with each other. We can be the two fools who can't dance but who are so in love, there's no one else but them on the dance floor. Okay?"

She nodded. "You know at first I thought you might like-like Alessandra."

Am I that easy to read? Shit. I need to work on my poker face.

"How so?" I raised my eyebrow slightly.

"Because she's dark and mysterious and..." her voice trailed.

I waited for a moment before egging her on. "And?"

"Probably more interesting, definitely prettier and...well, obviously, much younger."

I pursed my lips and lifted her chin, forcing her eyes to meet mine. "You're dark and mysterious, you're fascinating, so incredibly talented, the hottest girl I have ever met, and you're everything to me. There's a million Alessandras, Jens, Sophies, but there's only one you."

That's almost a hundred percent true. I think. Maybe. Yes. I love Caroline. I wouldn't throw that away for a little bit of mystery and intrigue.

I felt Caroline's doubt still resonating in her mind. I watched as she tried to search the ceiling for something to distract her.

My sweet little one, how charming and endearing you are. Let me take your mind to a more mysterious place.

I propped myself up onto an elbow as I turned her face toward mine. Kissing her supple lips, I ran my fingers down her arm, taking her hand in mine. She squeezed it in reply and a smile crept across her face. I brought myself to straddle her, pinning her hands above her head. She giggled and pulled against my hold as I kissed her neck.

"You're so ticklish," I cooed at her. "And you say I fidget." She smiled up at me. Her eyebrow raised as I reached for the bed restraints, pulling out the straps and undoing the Velcro cuffs. Leaving some wiggle room around her wrists, I tightened each strap against the bed, gently forcing Caroline's arms wide. I continued my teasing, nibbling her ears, kissing down her neck, down to her nipples. As I took one in my mouth, her breathing quickened, and I sucked a little harder. My hand slid to her throat, gently placing pressure around her, holding her head steady. I saw the corners of her mouth rise and I continued showering her breasts with nibbles and licks. I slid my knee between her legs, letting my thigh touch her bare slit, damp with arousal. I let my hand travel from her neck, between her breasts, to push her legs wider. I began to tickle her inner thighs ever so slightly with my tongue as she struggled against the bed ties.

"Shush," I whispered. She obeyed immediately, relaxing back into the pillow. Spreading her lips apart, I began to lick her clit, coaxing a build-up of sensations between her legs. Caroline moaned softly as I kept going, pressing my lips against hers more deliberately. I continued with her in my mouth until I heard Caroline beg a little.

"Please," she said, her soft voice barely audible.

I let my hand take the place of my mouth as I moved up her body, lying beside her. My fingers increased their pressure.

"I thought Mistress asked you not to talk." Her beautiful eyes met mine with a drunken, lustful wantonness. I knew I would cave eventually but I let my fingers tease her a little longer, as my mouth caressed her lips intensely. She eagerly kissed me back. My fingers teased inside of her, enjoying the hot and wet reaction they provoked. I found her G-spot, keeping my thumb on her clit, and massaged her until she couldn't return my kisses. She pressed her head into the pillow, her eyes closed as her body rushed into orgasm. "Should I let my little one cum?" I taunted sweetly. She attempted to nod as her hands instinctively grasped at the air, looking for something to take hold of. Her back arched as she let out a loud sigh of relief, embracing the passing flow of energy. I waited for her body to sink back into the mattress before I undid the restraints. She had a sweet expression of satisfaction on her face. She leaned into me and let her lips linger on mine. Straddling my leg under the covers, she tucked herself into the crook of my arm, placing a hand over my stomach.

"Thank you," she whispered, exhaling deeply.

I kissed the top of her head and stared at the ceiling, listening to her breathe. I could smell the rosemary-mint of her shampoo. As her breathing slowed peacefully, her slender body relaxed into the contours of mine.

Chapter Sixteen

I stepped out of the limo, holding my dress closed, extending a hand for Caroline who followed my footsteps. Allie was already on the carpet, posing for the hundreds of cameras in a stunning tango-inspired, orange gown with a train that flowed several stairs behind her. She looked back at us and waited for us to catch up.

"Miss Alessandra!" A distinct shout came from the crowd of cameras. She turned her head in the voice's direction. "Who are you wearing?" It was the moment that Caroline had been working toward for months, her ten seconds of glory that would hopefully catapult a career's worth of success. Allie took Caroline's hand as we caught up, leading her to stand beside her. "Black Magic by my good friend, Caroline."

Camera bulbs flashed ecstatically as the two women posed for a few more seconds. I waited in the wings and trailed behind them as Allie led Caroline up the stairs. Stepping into the Hollywood-inspired theater, we regrouped and collected glasses of wine and champagne. Francesco was already inside and called Caroline over, leaving Allie and me to mingle.

"I think Carol is happy," Allie whispered. "I hope you are too. I want you to be happy."

Why would you care?

I smiled and nodded as I took a sip from my glass.

"Thank you, yes, Caroline is ecstatic. She couldn't have gotten a better person to represent her on the carpet." I did my best to mask my confusion over her last comment.

"Are you happy?" she asked, slightly annoyed at my choice in ignoring her prior statement.

I looked at her, trying to decipher the question. "I am happy for Caroline."

She was about to say something else, but her attention was directed elsewhere by her agent. Over the past few months Allie had continued to take opportunities to meet the both of us for lunch or dinner, taking the time to join us when we went to Valentino's in-house shows, and making sure she was on the guest list for any VIP party Valentino hosted. Caroline thought it must be Francesco pushing her on us, but it seemed like too much effort for a celebrity to put in, even a personally unhappy celebrity.

Allie had taken to texting me at all hours regardless of topic. We had learned over the course of many meals that she was in an unhappy relationship with a guy by the name of Alan—an arrangement set up by her agent. Alan was the director of a Los Angeles production company. She was struggling with the cultural differences between Americans and Italians. Moreover, she had an immense issue with the boorish behavior of a man who was used to getting everything he wanted from a young woman. She would tell us stories of his constant infidelity and how his now fully-grown kids disrespected her constantly when their father wasn't around. The pair were engaged, but she constantly asked us what we thought she should do. Most recently, Alan had taken to bringing women home while Allie was there and asking for them to 'play' with one another. Allie wasn't having any of it and decided to leave the next day, using her movie premier as the excuse. I pitied her as I watched her cross the room to chat with another group of people.

How dire it must be to just be a pawn in a game. And for what? Guess that threesome is out.

"You look awfully glum," a deep voice came from behind. "You're at a party. You should smile." A warm hand embraced the small of my back.

I hate it when people tell me to smile.

Regardless, I smiled and turned around expecting to be repulsed by the man. My annoyance turned to glee as a familiar face greeted mine. "Josh! Oh, my goodness, it's been ages!" I gave him a one-armed hug, genuinely happy to see him.

"It has!" He gave me a kiss on each cheek. "I haven't seen you since, what? College. You look fantastic, as always."

I kept my sunny disposition. "As do you."

Even though you're forty pounds overweight and balding. What was it with men once they hit their peak that they all became overweight and lost their hair? I suppose hair is genetics but hit the treadmill once and awhile.

I continued with a smile on my face. "What are you doing here? Are you in the movie business now?"

He brushed the top of his head with his palm, seemingly a little self-conscious. "Yeah, actually I am. I decided to join as crew when I was still in school and now am finally directing documentaries."

I nodded. "Congrats, that's pretty exciting."

He took a sip of his drink. "Thanks, yeah, it's

pretty cool. You're with Valentino now, right?"

I nodded. "I work with their sub-design company, Black Magic. In finance though with some marketing aspects. Nothing terribly fancy."

"You look pretty fancy for being the numbers girl. You clean up nice." He raised his glass to my sleek, body hugging dress.

I laughed. "I can't breathe or eat, but sure, it does the trick."

He searched a little too obviously at my left hand, which I left stationed on my hip. "Married? Kids?"

I laughed a little. "Not yet, no." I tried to recall whether or not Josh knew I was bi. Probably not. "Are you still with Sharon?" I asked quickly, trying to deflect the attention.

"Married almost ten years now." He rolled his eyes. "Ten years too long though."

Too long for Sharon, for sure.

"Ten years too long?" I exchanged my glass as the waiter passed by.

He shrugged. "What can I say? I stay for the kids. Two of them. But the spark is long gone. I travel too much, I guess. Too much time on set working and not enough at home."

I pouted a little in sympathy. "You and Sharon were always so great together."

He shrugged. "Boredom maybe, but really I think we've just grown out of each other. We got married right after university. It was just too young."

I nodded. "I can see that."

"Hey, honey." I felt her hand graze my ass. "Sorry, Allie had me go chat up everyone she could think of."

I love her hands on me. She smells divine.

I kissed her on the lips briefly. "Hi, babe. No worries. This is Josh, one of my old college friends." I turned to him. The blank stare was a good giveaway that he had no idea of my sexuality. "Josh, this is my girlfriend, Caroline."

They acknowledged each other with an awkward handshake. I could see Allie waving for Caroline to return. "Babe, she's calling you back over."

"You should go, I'm good." She gave me another kiss and stole my glass as she left.

"Wow," Josh exclaimed, "I had no idea." He stole a glass for me off a passing tray. "Here." He handed me the glass of red. "Is that *the* Caroline, as in the designer for Black Magic? I've heard a lot of great things about her. Undoubtedly a beautiful woman."

I nodded, taking the glass from him. "Thank you. She is pretty amazing, as a designer and as a partner."

"I didn't think you'd marry a girl." He took a sip of champagne. "Especially an older woman."

I immediately came to her defense. "She's only a few years senior to me," I said a little too quickly. I minded my tone as I continued. "Love doesn't care about age. We're best friends and lovers—what more could I want?"

"I wish I had your taste in women," he joked. "And nice to hear you didn't rebut my marriage comment." He tried to wink but his face scrunched, making him look as if he were in pain.

"If I do marry, it'll be to her." I swirled my glass, watching a miscellaneous bubble rise to the surface. "There are other things I have to sort out first."

That is true. If I do marry, I can't imagine marrying anyone else but Caroline.

"Such as?" he asked curiously.

Like parents.

I let the question hang as the crowd was ushered into the seating hall, and I took the opportunity to evade the question. I found Caroline in the mass. "It was great to see you. Caroline is calling me over so I should go, but I hope you enjoy the film. Maybe we'll see you at the after party." I scampered off after a quick pat goodbye on his arm, joining Caroline and Allie in the crowd.

****

I had been dreading this trip. I stood in line to board our connection, hauling one too many bags, ready with my passport open to the photo page. I let Caroline go before me. I smiled briefly to the gate agent and followed Caroline down the ramp.

"It'll be fine," she tried to console me.

I rolled my eyes. "It'll be interesting to say the very least."

I am going to hate every single part of this. Hate it.

Caroline's line had taken off like wildfire after Allie's premier. Even five months later, it had been non-stop celebrity requests after the tango-inspired gown made headlines in all the top fashion magazines and was smattered across every tabloid paper. Caroline, in her true kind-hearted nature, had shared some of her spotlight with me, saying it was because of me that she found the creative energy for an awe-inspiring dress. I continued to refute the claim, but Francesco was very supportive of it and now saw us as a power of two for the brand. Black Magic had grossed twice the projected sales within its first three quarters and was on track to finish the year in a similar fashion. Caroline was ecstatic and living the dreams she had envisioned all her life. I was happy to go along for the ride and help where I could, ensuring the line's financial success.

All the celebrity attention had not spared us publication in North America, and our recognition immediately went global after the Paris fashion show. Bella Vita insisted on having the both of us featured on the front of the spring issue, due for release early February. It was the most in-depth article we had done so far, and so came the time whereby I could no longer hide on the other side of the world. It was time to face the parents.

It was the holiday season, so I almost had a guarantee that my mother would want to keep up appearances and not be one-hundred percent angry the whole time. Dad would be his charming self no doubt.

We settled into our seats and Caroline took my hand. "Parents love me." She smiled.

"They'll have to." I smiled back. I squeezed her hand a little harder.

Except my parents aren't normal per say.

As the plane lifted off, Caroline snuggled into my shoulder and put her headphones in. She was out like a light within minutes. I had saved some work for this leg of the trip in hopes that it would take my mind off the inevitable argument brewing. I stared at the cursor, trying to focus on the words I was supposed to will onto the page. I stared a little longer, taking a glass of terrible airplane wine for myself and for Caroline. Drinking both, I felt my eyelids getting a little heavier.

Quicker than I had anticipated, the airplane touched down, engines roaring, wheels skipping a little on the wet ground.

Caroline, hair still immaculate despite the flight, said, "I'm glad you slept finally."

I looked over at her. "Me too." I didn't feel any better really, but alcohol induced airplane sleep hardly ever made me feel perky.

"Here." She passed me the declaration card to sign.

"Thank you." I kissed her. It was a long walk through the airport to collect our bags, but I was in no rush. My feet felt like dead weights as I dragged them to customs.

Waiting in line at customs, Caroline looked at me, a little concerned. Taking my hand, she asked, "Your parents never offer to come get you?"

I shrugged. "It's hit and miss. I don't think I have ever accepted the offer. At this point it more feels like I'm putting them through such hassle, I just avoid it all together."

She nodded a little. "What about dropping off?"

I shook my head. "Twice—when I first left years ago, and never once have they offered since then."

"That's strange. Even Angela comes to get me if I'm coming to see her. Well, she gets her driver to drive her but still, she bothers to be there. She almost always drops me off too."

I shrugged. "Honestly, as sad as it is, I still look for them in the baggage hall when I get here. I've been trying to stop myself from doing that. It's been, what, six years? Maybe at the end of year seven, I'll have learned my lesson." I yanked the bags off the belt, and we made our way to the taxi line. I texted my mother an update of our arrival. She seemed relatively happy that I was back, but she kept her texting sentiments short.

It was almost dinner time locally, and we were

going to meet my parents in just over an hour. Practically stumbling into our hotel room with the abundance of luggage, we both quickly showered. My mind was elsewhere, my thoughts running away with themselves. We barely exchanged any words.

"What am I wearing for this?" Caroline started to unpack her dresses into the closet.

I cast a glance at the closet of clothes she had organized. "Well, it's still kind of raining so I plan on doing a pair of dark denim, booties, button down shirt, and a blazer. I can bring an umbrella if you'd like."

A little surprised, she questioned, "Really, that casual?"

"I'm not wearing ripped jeans," I offered. "I'll wear a flashy belt."

"Oh yes, the belt will make a world of difference." She waved a hand in dismissal. "How about this?" She held up a black and blue tartan dress. "With tights and boots?"

I nodded. "Perfect. You will look stunning." I felt my stomach churn as the minutes went by. The restaurant was only a five-minute walk away, but I felt like I needed to be there early, as if for a job interview. I waited impatiently on the bed, shaking my foot subconsciously.

"Jeez, you're making me nervous," Caroline said as she put on her coat. "Come on, let's go before you rattle your way through the floor."

We held hands, strides matching, as we made our way to the restaurant. We had thirty minutes to kill.

"Glass of wine?" I looked to Caroline eagerly. I would need something to make this easier.

She laughed, shaking her head. "Sure."

As I sat at a high-top table, the glass of vino in my hand seemed to disappear all too quickly. Caroline was trying her best to make small talk with me, but I wasn't being much of a conversationalist. My hands were a little clammy, and I wiped my palms on the side of my legs. It was five minutes to anticipated parental arrival, and Caroline went outside for a quick puff while I settled the drinks. I came to join her under the restaurant awning. I saw my mother first, fake smile ready for presentation. My father trailed behind her, looking somewhat genuinely cheerful. I sighed heavily and let out a little curse word under my breath. Caroline took my arm and stood beside me, increasing her grip around my forearm.

And here we go.

"Just us two," she whispered comfortingly.

Just us two.

"Hey, Mum," I called out. Forcing my own smile, I gave her a hug. "Hey, Dad." I gave him a one-armed hug. "This is Caroline." I cleared the path for their greetings.

Pleasantries were exchanged, and we headed inside to our table. I felt my mother's eyes drilling into my head as Caroline proceeded to make conversation with my father. The first few moments at the table were awkward. Incredibly awkward.

I offered a neutral question. "So, Mum, how's the garden?"

"It's winter. There's no gardening," she snapped, mouth in a thin line. She held a glass of ice water, bringing it to her lips with a very still hand.

I nodded. "Right, of course. How's Grandma?" I looked at Caroline, who was very intent on reading the menu. My father was watching whatever was outside.

My mother shot me a look of annoyance. I had a great relationship with my grandmother and was always much closer to her than to my mum. Grandma had all her wits about her, but her body was failing her. It wasn't easy for anyone. I called as often as I could, but it would always be a point of contention in my leaving. My mother softened a little. "She's a lot older now." She changed her tone. "You wouldn't know."

"I call every week," I protested slightly.

I got the dagger eyes again. "Calling is not the same as being there," she retorted.

This is going well.

My mother put down her water glass loudly on the table. "So, dear, I've read a lot about you and your friend here in the papers. That fashion line of yours seems to be doing well." Her tone was condescending, her body language stiff and unwelcoming. Her almost flattering statement made my heart pound harder. This was just the build-up.

"Yes, Caroline's line is doing very well." I shot a quick smile at her. Sympathetic eyes looked back at me.

Do I get in front of the train and try and stop it or just let it hit me?

My mother repositioned herself in the chair, leaning forward, lowering her tone, her eyes piercing mine. "There's also so much garbage in the press. They keep saying in the tabloids you two are actually together—as in lovers." My dad spat his drink back into his glass, snorting a little through his nose. Caroline looked at me out of the corner of her eye, still using the menu as a shield. My heart was about ready to pound itself out onto the table. My stomach was in my throat.

"You're not *lovers,* are you?" The disdain in her voice dripped with venom. "I didn't raise you this way." She leaned even farther over the table. "Are you or are you not?"

I'm a grown adult. Why do I still cower at this tone?

I tried to find my voice. I felt Caroline's hand on mine, and it gave me enough strength to stutter, "Yes, Mum, yes we are."

She sat back, a smug look on her face. "And with an older woman!" She shook her head. "I thought I had raised you right."

I felt tears beginning to form. My father sat there, entertained.

Hold it together.

"I love Carol—"

My mother cut me off and continued to spit her anger. "You don't know what love is. You're a foolish girl. You're a confused, foolish girl." She turned to Caroline. "I don't know you. You seem nice. I'm sure you're lovely, but you should know better. At your age, you should know much better."

Caroline sat up straighter in her chair, and her eye twitched a little. "I love your daughter. Nothing will change that."

Disgusted by Caroline's response, she turned back to me. "I hope you enjoy your time here. I don't expect her to come to Christmas dinner, but I will be expecting you. I don't want to disgrace the family with your foolish decision." She stood abruptly, putting on her coat. "Let's go. I don't want to eat here." She motioned for my father to follow her.

Hold it together until they leave.

I gripped Caroline's hand tighter.

My father stood. "Well, I can say it'll get better. Most likely anyway. Caroline, you're welcome to come to Christmas. If you make my daughter happy, then that's all that matters." He paused. "I had no idea, but I can see the allure." He winked at Caroline and then turned to look at me. "I'll talk to Mom." He gave me a pat on the shoulder, shook Caroline's hand, grabbed his jacket, and left.

The tears started rolling down my face as we sat in silence.

****

My nails clicked on the check-out counter, waiting impatiently for the in-training cashier to figure out my age on my driver's license. Caroline held the small of my back lightly, rubbing her thumb gently. Tapping my card on the reader, we left with the bottles in hand.

She did up her seatbelt. "You're sure about this?"

I started the car. "Babe, if I wasn't, it would mean I wasn't sure about you and me."

Caroline placed the two bottles into festive bags. "This won't go over well."

Shrugging, I looked at her. "Oh well, if it's any consolation, the rest of my family will be good with it."

"How do you know?" Caroline looked out the window, trying to hide the disbelief in her voice.

"Well, my cousin texted me this morning. He said he had heard the news and was very excited to meet you. My uncle and aunt texted similarly. Grandma doesn't text but I talked to her this morning and she's thrilled."

Caroline looked at me a little shocked. "Your mom has already spread the word?"

"Spread it like wildfire. She's just hoping that setting the tone and letting her viewpoint be known to the entire family will deter me from bringing up the subject."

"Or me."

"Doesn't matter. My family will really like you, don't worry. They'll have my back and yours." We drove the rest of the way in silence, holding hands. We pulled up to the house—we were not the first to arrive thanks to my thirty-minute delay.

My cousin gave me a head-nod as he was unloading gifts from his truck. "Hey, Coz!"

"Hey, Ty." I waved. I helped Caroline out of the car, and we gathered gifts from the trunk. Tyler came around to give me a hug. "Ty, this is Caroline."

He gave her a big hug. "So nice to meet you. Hope you brought extra alcohol for tonight! Family is all abuzz about you two. Don't worry, everyone already loves you...you know, besides the exception."

Caroline let out a relieved giggle. "Yes, I seem to be making headlines already."

Ty took some packages off my hands. He whispered in my ear, "She's a hottie, Coz. Seems nice too. Kat and I are happy for you."

"Thanks." I smiled. "I think I'll keep her," I said audibly enough for Caroline to hear. "Let's go and start the fun." I offered Caroline my free arm as we walked up to the house. The house was abuzz with people. The smell of turkey and stuffing filled the front hall. My dad came around the corner from the kitchen.

"Hello." He gave me a brief hug. "Here, let me take your coats. Hi, Caroline, glad you could make it." He shook her hand. "You can bring the wine into the kitchen. Your Mother is in there." He raised his eyebrows playfully. "Good luck."

I'm going to need more than luck for this.

I knew my mother would be relatively cordial, probably only making subtle, back-handed comments, but I also knew that there would be many sarcastic smiles and passive-aggressive comments to me. I just hoped Caroline wouldn't be present for those. We walked down the hall, hand-in-hand. My mother was pouring a drink for my uncle and raised her eyes to see us, quickly casting them down again.

"Well hello there." My uncle came and gave me a big hug then shifting his attention to my right. "And you must be Caroline." He gave her a big hug as well. "You are just stunning, but dare I say prettier in person than in the magazines! Hey! Beth! Come here, come meet Caroline."

My aunt came around the corner. "Oh, would you look at you! You're a doll. Isn't she a doll, Kev?" My aunt hugged Caroline tightly, excitedly yammering to her husband. She turned her attention to me. "Good for you, finally brought someone to dinner you actually like."

"Love," I corrected my aunt.

"Definitely love. I can see it already." Aunt Beth nodded hearteningly.

I felt my mother's eyes staring at me, and I turned reluctantly, leaving Caroline in the welcoming hands of my aunt and uncle. "Hey, Mum." I walked over to offer her a hug.

"Hello." She turned away from me, getting the bean casserole out of the oven.

Caroline came back over with two bottles and

placed the bags on the counter. "Everything looks so lovely," she offered my mother.

"Hello, Caroline," she responded icily. "Thank you for the wine. They can go on the table over there."

Caroline smiled as she moved the wine to its designated spot. "Thank you for having me."

My mother's gaze darted up. "I didn't have much of a choice, did I?" Her lips formed a sarcastic, thin smile. "Please, make yourself at home. Grandma is in the living room."

We both backed away from her to find refuge elsewhere with more welcoming family members. I spotted my grandma seated in a chair beside the Christmas tree, near the warmth of the fireplace. I went over and gave her a big hug. Her frail frame seemed even smaller than I remembered.

"You're too skinny," Grandma said as she slapped my thigh. "You don't eat enough."

I laughed at the familiarity of her statement. It was a dance we did every time we saw one another. "I eat a lot, don't worry." I smiled at her. "Grandma, this is Caroline."

Caroline bent down to hug her, crouching beside her chair. "Pleasure to meet you."

"Well, aren't you just the prettiest thing I have ever seen? You're not as pretty as my lovely granddaughter here, but you will do just fine!"

I rolled my eyes. "Grandma…"

Caroline smiled at me. "She is a very pretty girl. I'm the luckiest girl to call her mine."

Grandma leaned in a little to Caroline and me. "Do you think you could fetch me something good to drink? And maybe one of those cheese bites? Before your mother comes back?"

"Of course." I laughed. "I'll get it. Be right back." I left Caroline in the capable hands of Grandma. I watched as I poured Grandma a glass of Chardonnay. Caroline was very attentive to her. It made me smile.

The evening was going a little better than I had thought it would. Everyone showed sincere enthusiasm in meeting Caroline. Kat, recently engaged to Tyler, was excited to hear about Caroline's wedding dress designing. My two youngest cousins, both girls in high school, were in love with Caroline's new spring line. Caroline was the hit of the party. As dinner was wrapping up, I helped my mum in the kitchen.

"Seems that everyone likes her," she offered in disdain.

I nodded my head. "Seems that way."

She shifted her weight uncomfortably in her kitten heels. "I'm only tolerating this because your father relentlessly insisted."

"I figured as much." I looked at her, trying to maintain a confident appearance as I took the dessert platters out of the fridge. "Mum, I need you to get on board with all of this. I know it's a lot to take in right now, but I love Caroline and I know that won't change anytime soon."

Keep your face stern.

My mother looked at me in disgust. "You don't know what you want. You're just an irrational girl. This is just a phase." She breathed a deep breath. "And mark my words, I will never accept her or this whole"—she made a circle in the air—"*thing* you call a relationship."

My heart grew heavy. "I hope you change your mind someday."

Keep it together.

"I won't. Ever." She slammed the dessert forks on the counter. "Now," she changed her tone again, "go find out who wants tea or coffee." She offered a sarcastic smile and swept a stray strand of hair out of her face.

Unbelievable.

I did as I was bid and brought Caroline a black coffee, joining her on the living room couch. Keeping up our spirits, Ty and Kat came to sit near us.

"So, did you hear?" Kat asked me. "Caroline offered to design my wedding dress! I can't believe I'll have a designer gown!"

"Is that so?" I looked over at Caroline with a smile. How typical of her to offer. She would design everyone outfits if she could.

Caroline nodded. "I have a tailor here that owes me a favor, so I'll send her the design and Kat just has to go to the fittings."

Ty leaned over to me and quietly asked, "Designer usually means expensive. What should I be expecting?"

I looked over at Caroline who shook her head. "Nothing, Ty, don't worry about it. It's our wedding gift to you both."

"Really?" Tyler's face showed a huge sign of relief. "Thanks, you two."

Kat lit up and clapped her hands in excitement. "Oh thank you so much!" She hugged Caroline tightly. "This is so amazing! A designer gown, for me!"

"Isn't that nice of Caroline." My mother stood in front of us. "Here, these are for you." She passed me a few gift bags. "Receipts are inside."

"Thanks, Mum." I accepted the bags. "I put Dad's

and your gifts by your seats."

"Yes, I saw them, thanks." The awkward tension passed again as she left.

"Here, there's something inside for both of you," Aunt Beth said, handing me a box.

"Thank you, that's so sweet of you." I smiled at her. The card was addressed to both of us, so I handed it to Caroline. It was a mini-breakthrough for us both—a joint card and gift. While Caroline was occupied, I opened my mother's gift to me. Her written card was filled with standard holiday messages and very generic. Her gift was something I had talked to her about months ago and actually had wanted. I looked at the gift receipt. It had been purchased long before she would have gotten wind of Caroline's and my relationship.

Makes sense.

I sighed and put the gift and card back in the bag. I put on my best face and went to go hug my mother. She glared at me. "Thanks, Mum, I appreciate you getting me that. Really needed it." I stood waiting for a response. I waited a little more and was ignored.

Guess I'll go back to my seat now.

"Hey, Coz," Tyler called from behind. "This is awesome! How'd you know I wanted this?"

I genuinely smiled at his heroic attempt to save me. "Every hiker needs a good set of compact dishes. You're very welcome." I walked back to join Caroline, sitting beside her and placing my arm around her shoulders. I made every attempt to remain polite but avoid any additional contact with my mother. The evening concluded a couple of painful hours later. I closed the car door for Caroline as we finished saying goodbye to my family.

Kat tapped on the passenger window, which Caroline rolled down. "Thanks for coming tonight, Caroline. I know it can't have been easy. You're welcome in our house anytime."

Caroline gave a genuine smile. "Thanks, Kat. You and Tyler have been great."

"See you next time." Kat walked off, giving a little wave to us.

I rolled up the car window and backed out of the driveway. As we drove back to the hotel, the car was very quiet. I let the silence linger as I could tell Caroline was just as tired and stressed out as I was. We pulled up to the hotel and I let the valet take the car.

"Thank you for coming tonight." I kissed her forehead as the elevator climbed up to our floor.

She sighed. "Yeah, of course. I knew what I was getting myself into."

"Was it better or worse than you thought it would be?"

"I was super anxious the whole time and, holy cow, your mom doesn't let up, does she?"

I shook my head. "Now I think you can understand why I may have moved. It's a lot to handle when you put everything together. I needed to branch out and have some space." I opened the room door for her and felt a sudden sense of relief come over me. The hotel with Caroline felt more relaxing than the home I grew up in.

Caroline nodded. "To be honest, I'm glad I went but that was exhausting. Your cousins are pretty cool though, and your aunt and uncle are really nice people. Grandma is my favorite though, by far."

"Yeah, Grandma is awesome." I smiled, taking

Caroline's coat and hanging it in the closet.

I took off my jacket, not sparing any time in taking off the rest of my clothes. "I bet you're happy to be leaving tomorrow though."

"That was enough for me if you're okay with it." Caroline looked at me, doe-eyed.

"I'm okay with it, babe. More than okay."

****

We stood in line to board the plane to LA and I got the inevitable text from my mother.

—*Hi, thank you for helping at dinner last night. Caroline seems like a very nice person. But don't ever think that I will accept this relationship...or her as your 'life partner.' I hope you have a lovely time in LA, and I hope you get a better life perspective.*—

I immediately texted back.

—*Hey mum, thank you for a lovely Christmas dinner. Thank you for having us both. I don't see anything changing between Caroline and me. I hope you learn to accept it.*—

—*I will not. Stay safe.*—

"Mom texting you?" Caroline peered at my phone. "Fun things?"

I put my phone back into my pocket. "Very fun things. One day she will come around."

Maybe.

"We can hope." Caroline shrugged. "At the end of the day, we have one another, and if I make you happy, and vice versa, there's no reason to change things."

"Agreed. I love you and that won't change."

Chapter Seventeen

Caroline was adjusting the model's clothes as the hair stylist teased the back of the model's blonde locks. I watched the photo proofs on the computer screen as they came up. We were well into the fifth hour of shooting.

"How do they look?" Caroline came and peered with me.

"Fantastic." I smiled. "But do you like how the fabric is folding like that behind her knee?"

Caroline trotted off to fix the fabric folds and quickly came back. "Thanks for that."

"No problem. Babe, I need to call Francesco back and go grab a couple things. Can I meet you out front in a few hours?"

She nodded, taking a seat on my stool as I headed out into the late California sun. I loved Los Angeles, with the unconventional, almost all-year sunshine, and the odd societal expectation for everyone to be wealthy and to have an amazing body. As I observed the patrons at a few nearby shops it was almost as if living in a real-life reality show. I took a second to absorb my surroundings and collect my thoughts before lifting the phone to my ear.

The scene of my grandma and Caroline talking at Christmas crept back into my thoughts. Caroline had so delicately propped up her pillow, bringing her a blanket and hot tea when she had asked for it. It was the kind of attention only someone who was truly kind, caring, and warm-hearted would ever do. Caroline was so gracious about it all.

This is the perfect thing to do. Just us two after all.

"Francesco? *Ciao*, sorry I missed your call. I sent you the revised budget last night for Black Magic's bridal expansion. Did you get it?"

"*Si, buena*. Will have to get them signed off but I don't see any issue with it."

"Okay, great. *Grazie*."

"I've seen the marketing strategy as well. I know you told Gina to hold off, but I asked her to show me."

I rolled my eyes. "Of course she showed you. Those plans weren't done."

Francesco huffed on the other end of the line. "You are the most well-prepared strategist I've met. I like the concept. I added some notations and I will send it back by day's end."

"Sounds good." There was a momentary pause. "One more thing, would you mind if I stole Caroline tonight? I have a surprise for her."

I heard him smiling on the other side. "*Si*, no problem, I won't harass either of you. Hope the surprise goes well. *Ciao*."

"*Ciao, ciao*." I smiled too as I hung up. I dialed another number.

"You've reached the Dream Escape Excursions front desk, this is Amy. How can I help you?"

"Hi, Amy, we spoke earlier about a private rental for two on the Lucy Dreamliner? I wanted to confirm our appointment for this evening."

"Yes, I have you here for two guests. All the

preparations have been made accordingly."

"Lovely, thank you."

It was two hours until go-time and I still had to run a very important errand. I walked up the street to the florist.

"Hello, can I help you?" the lady behind the counter called out.

"Hi, yes, we spoke earlier. Order number ninety-seven," I said, showing her the receipt for the prepaid flowers.

"Yes, yes, I have your order in the back. Give me a minute." After a few minutes the florist brought out an enormous bouquet of red and white roses. "Two dozen red, and two dozen white long stem roses, and here's what used to be a bouquet of twenty-four red and white roses but are now just a bag of petals." The florist seemed a little off-put that I had asked for just petals as she plunked them into a carry bag for me.

"Thank you," I said, struggling with the overflowing number of roses in my arms. I made my way back to the studio, careful not to be visible to any of the studio members, and peered through the window. I saw that the shoot was wrapping up and Caroline was busy chatting with a crew member. Sneaking through the back door, I went to the dressing room, laying the flowers carefully down on the table. I rummaged through the crew locker I had snagged upon arrival and pulled out an extra change of clothes and shoes for each of us. I changed into a black pantsuit, sequined white top, and black Valentino stilettos. I looked at myself in the mirror—my long hair wasn't as disheveled as usual, but I ran through it with a brush hurriedly. It would have to do. I tucked in my shirt again, centering the buckle of my belt once more. I jotted down a note for Caroline to adorn the sequined white dress I had hung and the rose-colored heels beside it and then asked her to meet me out front. I walked out of the studio quickly, and as casually as I could muster with an armful of roses.

"Ms." The limo driver bowed his head a little as I approached. "My name is Sam, and I will be your driver for the remainder of the evening."

"Hey, Sam, pleasure to meet you." I peered over the floral arrangement at the portly gentleman in a well-tailored suit. "Would you mind scattering these rose petals inside for me?" I handed him the bag of red and white rose petals. My heart started to race.

My phone buzzed. I struggled to get it out of my pocket. It was Caroline.

—Where are you?—

—Outside, waiting for you.—

In growing anticipation, my heart thudded harder in my chest. I took a deep breath as I stood by the limo, roses in arm, the warm sun still hovering over the tree line. I adjusted my belt a little and tucked in my shirt for the third time.

The doors opened as Caroline stepped through. She looked like an angel in that moment, sun glistening off the dress, her hair flowing in the warm breeze. Her eyes met mine and bubbled with joy.

My God, I love this girl.

"What's this?" Caroline smiled ear-to-ear as she trotted over to me. Her eyes sparkled with curiosity. "What are you up to, my dear?"

"My lovely Caroline." I kissed her passionately on the lips, knowing full well her red lips would impart themselves on mine. She kissed me again, dancing her tongue on my lower lip.

I love the way she tastes. I could kiss her for hours.

Almost forgetting the gargantuan bouquet in my arms, I bluntly stated, "These are for you." She kissed me again, and I waved my hand to the open door. "Please, your chariot awaits." I let her step into the car. Sam had done a very good job of spreading petals throughout the car. Champagne lay ready for popping as it sat on ice.

"What is all of this?" Caroline asked, smelling her roses. Her smile was playful, and her eyes intrigued. I grinned at her as my heart began to settle a little. I took her hands in mine and kissed the tops of them.

"I wanted to show you how much I love you and how proud I am of you." I reached for the champagne. "You are the most important, most amazingly talented, most lovely, kind-hearted person I know. You deserve to be recognized."

She broke eye contact with me momentarily as a bit of color came to her cheeks. "Aw, Baby, thank you." She looked back into mine with the windows to her soul open. "Cheers to that, but I hope you know I feel the same way." She took my free hand and squeezed it tightly. "You're the first person I have ever truly loved and trusted. You are my world."

We managed to finish a glass before the privacy divider went down. "We're here, ladies," Sam informed us. "I'll see you in a few hours."

"Thanks, Sam." I took Caroline's hand once again. "Come on." I smiled at her. "It's time for your surprise." I opened the car door and the marina air kissed our faces. Two crew stood waiting at the end of the boat ramp, ready for our arrival. The vessel was trimmed in clear lights and subtle touches of red and white. I held Caroline by the small of her back as we crossed the walkway and boarded the yacht. Her dress swayed softly against the curves of her body. I couldn't help but stare at her perfectly shaped ass.

"Wow, this is amazing." Caroline looked at me, clearly intrigued.

I know, your ass is amazing.

Collecting myself, I said, "It gets better." I smiled.

A fair-haired lad helped us off the ramp, and we were escorted to the bow of the boat and each handed another glass of champagne. It wasn't long before the anchor was lifted, and we made our way slowly into the open water. The salt air was refreshing, and the gentle sway of the boat calmed my nerves a little more.

Suddenly, I knew what I had wanted to express so many times before but failed to find the right words. I let my mouth blurt it out. "I have a confession." I looked at her.

She eyed me curiously. "What's that?"

"I've been holding back when it comes to us." My heart began to race again, unsure of how Caroline would react to such a statement.

She took a sip of champagne, keeping an eye on me. "What do you mean?"

I took a deep breath. "You and I both have trust issues, for good reason, but I have come to realize that I trust you more than anyone." I paused. "And I've been thinking about how we are together, even behind closed doors, and I think I can do better."

She raised her eyebrows flirtatiously. "Better how?"

"I mean, I think I truly trust you enough to let myself, you know, get there." Caroline looked at me very confused. "I don't know how to get off with someone else, but I want to try. Is that okay?"

Caroline smiled sweetly. "Oh, honey, we have years to figure it out. No rush for us." She took a sip of champagne and took a moment to think. "So, along the same lines, do you think you would be comfortable being a little more Dominant with me?"

I was a little taken aback with the request. "I can be. I'm just scared to do something you don't like."

"I will tell you," Caroline said as she took my hand in hers. "I trust you to hear me."

The boat was in open waters now, making its way along the coastline. The air was still warm from the day. I heard light footsteps behind us and a soft clearing of a man's throat.

"Pardon me, ladies, but dinner is ready to be served. Please follow me." The crew member led us to the top deck. A table for two had been fixed—arranged with an oversized white tablecloth, silverware, and glasses that were perfectly set. A bottle of red lay chilling in a polished silver ice bucket. He and another young man pulled out our chairs as we sat down.

Caroline looked at me, gesturing with her hands at the table and at her surroundings. "This is amazing. I don't even know when you would have had time for all of this."

I smiled at her as I waited for the server to open and decant the bottle for us. I had picked one of our favorite reds, native to California. "One must make time for the ones they love." I paused, taking in another deep breath, willing for my heart to calm down. I looked at her stunning green eyes, twinkling in the yacht's gentle deck lights.

I could get lost in those eyes every day.

I collected myself as the waiter poured our glasses. I looked up at the young man and nodded in thanks.

"Caroline," I started, my voice cracking ever so slightly, "I love you more than words can express. You are my entire world, and I wouldn't have it any other way." I swallowed as I saw the server reappear. "I would love for it to be that way for the rest of my life."

"As do I, my love." Caroline took my hand across the table. "I want to spend the rest of my life with you too."

The server came by. "Your first course, ladies." He placed down the plates. A black box sat on both our plates, tied up in white satin ribbons.

"What's this?" Caroline looked up at me with a raised brow.

I smiled. "Open it."

She undid the bow quickly and lifted the lid. Red tissue lined the box, folded neatly with a gold seal. Caroline smiled as she carefully lifted the seal. Out of the box she lifted a set of rose gold handcuffs.

"These are so pretty." She rubbed her fingers along the smooth metal and looked at me inquisitively. "Don't you usually use rope on me?"

My mouth turned upward. "They're not necessarily for you. They're for you to use on me."

She cocked her head slightly. "You don't like being tied up. I thought you get panic attacks."

"I want us to try. I think I'm ready…I know I trust you enough to let you. If it doesn't work out, I will use them on you. Deal?"

She giggled like a little girl. "Deal. Thanks, baby."

I blew her an air kiss. "Here," I said, handing her the box from my plate. "This one is for you too."

She looked at me with a frisky smile and started undoing the second box. "What's in here? A golden anal plug?"

I shook my head silently as she lifted out a white note card. She started reading through the note. Her eyes started welling with tears. "I mean every word of it. I can't imagine my life without you." My heart pounded loudly in my chest. "Is there anything else in there?" I stood and came beside her, crouching down on one knee, placing my hand on her bare thigh.

So soft. I love these legs.

She dug a little deeper into the tissue and pulled out a little red velvet box. I looked up at her from my one-kneed position. "Caroline, you are my best friend, the person I can spend every day with, the one I can talk to about everything, and someone I trust wholeheartedly. You and I have fun just being us, no matter where we are. I love you with all of my heart, and I would be the luckiest woman alive to ask you to be my partner in crime, my lover, and wife for the rest of our lives." I opened the box for her and held it in my palm. "Will you do me the honor?"

She burst into tears. "What..." she mumbled almost inaudibly. "What about..."

I placed the ring box on the table, careful not to dislodge the three-carat diamond from its slotted cushion. "I love you, Caroline. Regardless of anyone else's thoughts or opinions, I know I want you in my life forever." I reached up and took her face in my hands. I planted a kiss firmly on her lips. "I love you, so much."

"Yes," she whispered. "I would love to be yours. Forever." She smiled and snuggled into my shoulder, tears still streaming down her face. "I love you."

I kissed her again, letting my lips linger on hers. Our lips broke their connection when we simultaneously couldn't help but grin with sudden excitement. I placed the sparkler on her ring finger.

"You know something?" she said as she looked down at her new accessory.

I held her hand in mine. "What's that, babe?"

"I never thought that I would get proposed to. I suppose as a lesbian, it's a toss-up." She smiled broader, raising her hand before her face. "Honey, honestly, this thing is huge. It's absolutely stunning."

I poured her some more wine as I got back into my chair. "Here's to us, my love. I'm glad you like it. I couldn't find one anywhere that spoke to me, so I got that one made for you. The diamonds and stones are from two collections."

She looked at me, intrigued, as the waiter put down our actual first courses. "Which collection?"

"I have a friend who works at Tacori and handles their limited-edition, 'appointment only' rings. That one is two rings made into one. The two stones on either side of the diamond are actually taaffeite and come from an Italian heiress who donated her collection. They're considered much, much rarer than diamonds. The solitaire is from a nineteen twenty-one Tacori pendant made for a French actress. There's no other ring in the world like this one."

Caroline admired the ring as it danced in the light, then her demeanor changed as if suddenly being assaulted by a thought.

I looked at her expression of worry. "What just crossed your mind?"

She sighed heavily. "Your mother is going to flip."

I laughed a little, brushing the comment off with a flick of my wrist. "That's the understatement of the year. The deal was that I had to tell her about us, not that she had to like it." I smiled at her. "She'll come around...eventually. On the bright side, Grandma will be thrilled, as will everyone else."

Caroline nodded as she sipped from her glass. Taking my hand in hers, she smiled amiably. "Thank you for making this night so perfect. The yacht, the lights, the roses, the surprise, everything—I couldn't have imagined anything more romantic."

"You deserve this and so much more."

Chapter Eighteen

"Congratulations!" Francesco yelled loudly as we entered the studio. He started clapping and everyone else followed suit with the room erupting with cheers and whistles.

I looked at Caroline who looked back at me, a little surprised. Knowing that Caroline liked her privacy, as did I, my only available response was to shrug and state, "I didn't say anything, I swear." Caroline's cheeks flushed a little, so I placed my hand on her back, providing more emotional support than physical.

"Champagne!" Francesco continued with exuberance, rushing over to give us each a hug. "It's about time, ladies! Oh, this is perfect timing! Right at the launch of your bridal line!" He held Caroline's hands and swung her arms like a preschooler. "Oh! Do let me see the ring!"

Everyone in the studio came to see the sparkler, forming a little swarm around Caroline. I stepped out of the group as my phone started buzzing. "Hello?"

"Is it true? Francesco just texted me," the woman asked bluntly.

That guy can't keep quiet for a second.

I replied just as frankly, "Is what true, and who is this?"

"This is Stephanie Miller, Bella Vita's Content Editor," she said, sounding rather annoyed. "Your engagement to Caroline, is it true?"

"News sure travels fast, and yes, it is true."

"Great. Congrats. We want to do an exclusive story with you two and do a spread for the Black Magic bridal line launch. This will of course accompany the twenty-page spread we have already allocated for. It has to be done by the end of next week. I will send you all the details. Does that work for you?"

"Okay."

"Good, you'll receive details within the hour. Email me if you have questions." With that she hung up.

Caroline walked over, handing me a mimosa. "Who was that?"

I couldn't help but let out a chuckle in disbelief. "Bella Vita. They already heard about us and want to do an exclusive story for the bridal launch using us as the subjects in addition to what we had planned with them." I saw Caroline hesitating, so I continued, "I know we're not ones for the spotlight but, PR wise, it would be amazing for the line."

She shrugged, rather unwillingly. "I suppose you're right. You think Francesco will be okay with it?"

I squeezed her hand. "Who do you think sent the news flash?"

She rolled her eyes. "Of course, that makes perfect sense."

"Did you say yes?" Francesco came over, even more excited than before. "They called, didn't they?"

"We said yes." I smiled. "I don't know how they knew so quickly though." I gave him a little nudge and raised my glass. Caroline's demeanor changed suddenly, remaining silent beside me. Her mind had wandered elsewhere.

Francesco didn't seem to notice. "*Bella, bella, bella,* we must all make sacrifices to get ahead," he joked. "This will be fantastic. Did she send you the details yet? I heard they want to shoot it in New York."

I shrugged. "Maybe, haven't heard yet."

"So, I was thinking…" Caroline broke her silence, and looked at the two of us. "If we're going to do this whole Bella Vita shoot thing, I need to do something different."

"Different, babe?"

All I got was a nod in response before Caroline was picking out fabrics from the wall and draping it over a model. Francesco trotted over to get more champagne and orange juice, going to stand by her, exchanging mutters.

"What am I doing?" Caroline announced abruptly to the room. "You, honey, come here. This is for you after all."

I made a face of slight displeasure. "Oh boy. Really, Caroline?" I begrudgingly made my way over and took off my blazer.

"You'll need to take off more than that. Here, put this bustier on." She slapped my ass flirtatiously. "And tie up your hair, please, my love."

I changed behind the room divider and came out in the very limited clothing Caroline had provided, earning a couple looks from the women in the room.

"Me-ow," Francesco said, making a little claw motion in the air. "If I was into chicks, I'd do you." He elbowed Caroline in the ribs. "Good pickings, Carol. You're going to have a lot of fun with that."

She winked at him in response. "Don't I know it.

You should see her with nothing on at all." I felt Caroline pinch my ass, teasing me.

I felt my cheeks begin to flush. "Just wait until it's your turn for this part."

"We're basically the same size. You'll be doing both of ours until the final fittings."

"I have other things to do, you know," I protested. "The line's budget, marketing strategy to work out with Bella Vita now, plan..."

Francesco looked at me. "What our lovely Carol needs, she gets. Just no quickies behind the divider," he kidded, "or if you do, at least lock the door."

Carol's needs...

I smiled to myself.

Damn this thing is itchy.

I itched under the ribbing of the bustier.

"Hey now, just you hold on a second, Babe." Hoping my traditionalist point would provide an escape from my current situation, I retorted, "Isn't there some rule where the bride and bride can't see each other in each other's dresses?"

She rolled her eyes dramatically. "We're lesbians—well I am, you're bi and committing to the 'dark side', so aren't we breaking ancient traditional rules as it is?"

White fabric fluttering all around me, Caroline's assistant cut where indicated.

I pushed a little harder. "Do you really want to lose that element of surprise?"

"Okay, okay, we will figure it out, but for now, just hold still." Caroline's tone was a little barky as she gathered fabric around my waist. "You're so fidgety."

My phone dinged. "It's that Bella Vita email." I

began to scroll through.

"Babe, quit moving." Caroline slapped my arm.

"Give, give, here, I'll read it." Francesco took my phone much to my dismay and reluctance to hand it over. "Okay, wow!" His voice was getting overly-excited again. "They're really going overboard with this. It's a New York shoot. Oh this is good—they're closing out Tiffany's, Central Park, and the Empire State Building top lookout point."

"Sounds cute," I offered. "A little typical, but okay. I think I can do better."

Francesco snorted. "It's your funeral," he said, handing me the phone. "Give it your best shot. God knows you've done wonders for us."

I smiled at the compliment. "I'll see what I can do." I took back my phone and formulated a response, trying to keep my arms out of the way of Caroline's assistant.

Delayed in reaction as Caroline was fumbling through her sketches and a little distracted, she asked, "What did they say? Is the shoot up to your standards?" Caroline looked at me rather puzzled and with a multitude of trimmings in her hands. She started draping certain ones against the fabric folds.

"It was okay—fairly standard, a New York love theme. A classic tale, which is sweet, but I think I can do better." I pressed the send icon, and my phone swooshed in response.

"Go for it. I trust you over them any day," she said, pinning fabric around my bust.

****

The weather in New Jersey was favorable this afternoon. Bella Vita had specifically requested to do the shooting in New York, but with my staging requests it was recalculated that the standing set in Jersey was more appropriate.

"The lovely couple has arrived." The announcement was made as if we were a part of the royal family. We were guided to separate rooms by a fairly juvenile stagehand. "Your designated dresses are in the room per Caroline's instructions. Stephanie will meet you in the studio in an hour. My name is Eddie, if you need anything." With that, Eddie, the assistant, quickly left.

"See you on the other side, babe." I kissed her goodbye as we went to our respective rooms. A petite red-headed girl was waiting for me, makeup brushes in hand, readying the space. Her blue eyes shot out from her face like arrows. My sudden attraction to her hit me as ferociously as a semi-truck.

Ah, shit. Deep breaths.

"Hi, my name is Daniella." Her hand was strong as she took mine. "I'll be doing your hair and make-up today." She hesitated. "Please take off your clothes…" She paused, letting the sentence linger. "Behind the divider there's a robe for you, and a pair of heels."

Why am I attracted to her? I shouldn't be. I made a commitment to someone I truly love.

My response came out like a racehorse from its starting gate. "Usually women let me take them on a first date before I take my clothes off." I couldn't help but grin coyly at her.

Shut up, behave, you're engaged.

I looked at her from head to toe. Her hair was curled loosely, pinned up with a butterfly clip. Daniella wore a dark, ripped jean skirt and a purple and black, polka dot top with waist peplum. She was a vertically challenged girl, even in her six-inch, black platform heels. Up and down her left arm she had a mélange of tattoos and a double piercing in the helix of her right ear. I did as I was bidden and tied the robe securely, a little too securely, around my waist and came to sit in the director's chair in front of the mirror. I watched as she took a brush to my hair. She was gentle with each stroke.

I like those tattoos. Why am I such a sucker for a girl with tats?

Being that it was just the two of us in the room I decided I should make some small talk. "So, Daniella, how long have you been doing this for Bella Vita?"

"Three years." Her accent was strong—she sounded Eastern European perhaps. She ran her fingers under the neck of my robe, gathering the fine hairs. I shuddered a little. "Sorry, are my hands cold?"

I didn't lift my eyes, knowing hers would be looking back at me in the mirror.

"No, no, you're just fine," I responded quietly.

Too fine. Damn it. Shut up. Her hands know how to handle themselves. I want...just be quiet.

"Have you always been in this line of work?" I tried to be as casual as I could, desperately attempting to drown out the thoughts in my head.

Our eyes met in the mirror and she held my gaze, keeping her hands steady. The corners of her mouth turned upward slightly, as if knowing what I was thinking.

Dangerous.

She proceeded to answer the question. "I started back home in Poland, but there isn't much work there for my type of work. I moved to Moscow for a couple years, but the working environment isn't so fun, so I moved here seven years ago and slowly made my way to this job. I have a friend who helped me out." She became a little more talkative as she grew immersed in her work. "It's better here." Daniella took the ends of my hair and put them into curlers, spraying them into place.

I couldn't help but prod a little more. "Do you have any family here?"

She came around the front of my chair, placing one leg between mine, a little farther between than necessary. "I will do your make-up now, okay? Your hair needs to stay put and dry."

I nodded and felt her bare leg brush against mine. My robe fell to the side, exposing my upper thigh.

She continued, appearing to ignore the sudden connection of warm flesh. "No, I have no family here. They are all back home." She sounded a little melancholy. "I haven't seen them since I left."

"That's a long time for you. You must miss them."

"Look up," Daniella said as she applied mascara to my bottom lashes. "I miss them. I have a cat now. I wanted a dog but they're too much work. And a roommate, I have one of those too." She shrugged. "One day I will go back." She cast her eyes down, taking a moment to adjust her legs to blatantly straddle mine. "Look down," she instructed, conveniently applying more mascara. I followed her instruction and ended up having the choice of looking at our touching thighs or looking straight down her top. I wanted so desperately to move my gaze, feeling I had been coerced into this somehow.

"Keep still," she whispered. "Do you always fidget this much or is there something wrong?" I didn't say anything, hoping the question would disappear. She reached for a brush on the table. "Lips time. Part them slightly for me."

She drew liner onto my bottom lip, and I didn't know where to look. Too scared to look into her sapphire eyes, too worried that if I looked down, I would get overly aroused by her tits. But if I closed them, it would seem weird. I tried looking through her—that seemed like the safest option.

"I make you nervous?" Daniella smiled coquettishly, pushing her leg into mine. Her jean skirt rose up farther, enabling me to feel her heat. "I think I can tell." She finished with the lip color, placing the brush back. "Why do I make you nervous?" She dusted a layer of bronzer onto my chest, pushing the satin robe open farther.

Her bluntness threw me off, my suddenly exposed chest making me feel vulnerable. I had no way of avoiding the question other than being overt. "So, you mentioned you had a cat? What's its name?"

She raised an eyebrow at my attempt to change the subject. "Her name is Estella. What about you, do you have any pussy…cats?" Daniella moved around to fix my hair once again, undoing the curlers. She maintained steady eyes on my loosened robe.

Oh goodness.

"I don't have any of the four-legged kind, but…"

Daniella started undoing my hair and moved a curl to the front of my shoulder, loosened it over my breast, running her hands through it, ever so slightly brushing over my nipple. My body betrayed me as my nipple became erect at the touch. In the mirror I watched as Daniella leaned over my shoulder, her ass perfectly shaping her skirt, her front exposing cleavage to me, pushing it out farther with a deep breath. I felt myself getting hot for her. I could feel her breath against my ear. I sat seemingly frozen as her lips traveled up my neck, to my ear, her teeth nibbling my earlobe.

Fuck. Fuck. Fuck. No.

I closed my eyes for a brief second, collecting my senses. "Daniella, I'm sorry, I can't. You know I'm with Caroline," I continued to protest. "We're engaged."

"But you can," she cooed, coming around to face me. She stood between my legs, running her nails up under my robe along my thighs. "I've heard what you can do to a woman. The industry is small." She winked. "I promise I won't tell a soul."

Another thing to hate Sophie for—her big, fat mouth—and Jen for telling her.

I stood abruptly, almost knocking over the chair. "Daniella, you are a stunningly beautiful girl but, no, I love Caroline, and I will not do anything to hurt what we have. You must understand."

Daniella was about to rebut but there was a knock at the door. "It's Francesco, *bella*. Are you almost ready?"

"*Si, si*, yes, we are almost done. Just letting out my hair."

"Caroline is getting fitted already. Hurry it up. I'll send in the other girl to help." A moment thereafter, another girl came in, saving me from the awkward situation that would have been. The mousy, black-haired young lady, with large rimmed glasses, brought in a dress labeled "Jones Dress One."

Her bossiness was unexpected. "Let's go, ladies, we don't have all day." She cast Daniella a dirty look as she motioned to the time on her watch. Turning her attention toward me, she handed me the gown. "Step into this, would you?" I nodded as she went to go hang it on the wall hook. I was careful to undo my robe while facing away from Daniella.

"Daniella, stop fussing with the brushes. Finish taking out her curlers. We have a schedule to keep."

A few moments later, I stepped into the elaborate corset gown. It was like taking a step back into the Renaissance era but with modern elements—an abundance of individually sewn crystals on the top layer of tulle. The corset itself was semi-transparent, accentuating the boning structure and the ribbon ties at the back.

"Suck it in," she said, pulling the ribbons tightly around me, cinching in my waist and overly accentuating my cleavage. I held onto the back of the chair as she took every last millimeter of space left. "Aren't you glad you don't have to try and eat in this?" She smiled, fastening the bow. I managed a nod as I tried to push out my ribs and regain some breathing room. She covered my shoulders to protect the dress as Daniella hovered around me, massaging the locks and spraying things into place. I watched in the mirror as she lingered a little too long on my rounded breasts. The mousy girl was growing even more impatient. "Do you have your shoes on?"

"I have a pair on," I said, showing her.

She grunted in dismay. "Wrong ones. Ugh, Daniella, really? Okay, here, put these in," the stylist said, passing me two crystal drop earrings. "You look like a modern-day Cinderella. Okay, Daniella, you're done with the hair. Go fetch the proper shoes. They want the white platforms over there." She pointed to the shoe wall. "No, not those. The pair of Dior, top right."

Daniella didn't say much but quickly retrieved the shoes, helping me change into them. She did them up painfully slowly, lingering on the buckles.

"Daniella!" Mousy barked at her. "They're waiting. Come, come, Ms. Jones, here, take my hand."

I stood in my overly tall shoes, gaining my footing, taking Mousy's hand for balance. She led me to the photo studio outside where the first scene was arranged. I was so focused on not tripping over the immense layers of fabric in my overly tall shoes, I didn't notice Caroline at first, who stood off to the side as the lighting crew adjusted the overhead filters.

"Wow," I heard her say as I approached.

I looked up at her. She was in a flouncy, ivory tulle, tea-length dress with a lavish amount of red crinoline poking out from underneath. The sweetheart neckline framed her breasts voluptuously. Paired with a pair of classic red, platform Louboutins, she looked like a fresh take of a nineteen forties bride.

"You look absolutely adorable." I gave her an air kiss. "I hope you like these spreads." I had kept the plans a secret, only gaining Francesco's approval in the designs.

"Ms. Jones, the director wants to have your input," Mousy said, fiddling with her glasses.

"Absolutely. Excuse me, babe." I took a look at the set. It was almost identical to the drawings I had done. Set left was an eighteen-foot-high green screen. In front sat a twin engine, nineteen-forties propeller plane. Set right were three brown and tan Buicks from the same era. The weather had decided to cooperate today with clouds covering most of the sun's rays. The rain machines above were ready for use.

Francesco came over to me. "This is a risky one, *bella*, but I'm sure it'll be a great spread."

The mousy girl came back. "I think we're ready. Director, do you want them to take their positions?"

The director pointed at me. "I'm just here today for creative support. It's her show."

I laughed. "Hardly. I just drafted this scene. You're the master."

I heard Caroline snicker beside me. "First and last time I'll hear that," she muttered under her breath. I grinned at her coquettishly.

"Yes, right, okay. Caroline, dear, please take your spot by the third car." Mousy really became the boss at this point. "Caroline, here are your first props," she said, handing her the Portobello fedora and tan blazer. "Daniella, please help her with it and for goodness sakes, hurry it up." She turned to me. "Dear, here is your Casablanca fedora and trench." She turned to Daniella, who was still fussing over Caroline's locks. Shaking her head, she helped me on with my hat.

I took my designated position in front of Caroline and swung the trench coat over my shoulder. The scene didn't have to be an exact replica, and nor would it be.

"You ladies look fantastic. Wait there. Caroline should have a small leather clutch. Eddie, where's the Hermes clutch I asked you to bring? Eddie!" She looked around, obviously annoyed at this point. "Where's that damn assistant when you need him?" she asked herself under her breath. The young, twenty-something appeared. "Eddie, there you are. Go find the Hermes clutch in props. Daniella, come fix her lip liner." He scampered off as Daniella came over to me.

"You look very pretty. Caroline looks even better." Daniella winked. "Don't worry, I still like you best." All I could do was stare at her and try and make my eyes into daggers as the brush outlined my lower lip.

"Okay, Daniella, finish up. Caroline, take your place again, please." Mousy scampered back to the screen and pointed at something, mumbling to the director, "Can we have more light on Carol please?"

Flashes went off dramatically. "Softer lenses on camera one please," said the director.

"Let's set the scene before we make it rain. Caroline, you're about to leave on that lovely rickety plane over there, and you can't bear to leave but you must. The moment is heartfelt longing, and let's make sure to play up the romance in the scene. Okay, one more round of test shots." Cameras went off again, as Mousy watched closely as the proofs came up on the director's screen. They seemed to nod in contentment. "Make it rain!" At her command, the fictitious skies opened up above us and the water came down in what felt like sheets of rain.

After what seemed like an eternity of posing and making minor changes in the heaviest downpour imaginable, Mousy spoke up. "Camera two? Who's camera two? Is that you, Marina? Careful you're not catching shadow from the set. Individual close-ups, please."

I wanted so badly to rip the lace from my chest and scratch my skin where the lace had teased and rubbed, only made worse by the accumulation of moisture. By now the dress corset had molded around my ribcage and I was beginning to feel a bit claustrophobic. I looked at Caroline, who smiled kindly back at me, and I couldn't help but forget about my aching ribs and fall in love with her all over again. It was time for the second change. I had a quick rush of panic set in. I didn't want to deal with Daniella again.

"Hey," I called out to Mousy, realizing I still had no idea what her name was. "Would it be okay if I handled the wardrobe change on my own? Daniella was great but…" I let my voice trail off.

"A little too 'in your face'?" Mousy asked.

I nodded. "A little."

She shook her head, exasperated. "Not an issue. I'll send in someone else. Don't worry, I won't ask her to see Carol either."

"Thanks, appreciate it." I smiled at her understanding.

I changed into my next gown, with a shy, young seamstress helping me. The blush, slim-fitting dress had a plunging neckline and open back. A waterfall of crystals swung from the shoulder straps and tickled my lower back. I hadn't seen this one in Caroline's line-up of dresses before, but it was definitely a favorite. Putting on a simple Dior stiletto, the girl dried and adorned my hair with little crystal and floral accents and sprayed the ringlets in place.

I walked to meet Caroline on set. This scene was luckily not in the midst of a downpour. The set's balcony was adorned in vines, and various red roses that crawled their way up the grand stone façade toward the Juliette balcony. A ladder had been placed among the foliage to cover the ten-foot drop.

"Here." Eddie passed me a red rose.

I took my place on the ladder, rose in hand, reaching the top to meet Caroline, who greeted me with a wide grin. "I'm excited to kiss you." She giggled.

I looked at her endearingly. "You get to kiss me all the time."

"Not nearly enough." She leaned over the railing and gave me a peck on the lips. Unexpectedly, cameras went off despite the spontaneity of the shot.

It was a whirlwind six-hour session, four wardrobe changes each. I was utterly exhausted. Francesco seemed satisfied as to how things had turned out. He figured the spread would make a big enough splash for the line that it would make reprint in all the magazines that could afford to publish it. We wouldn't know until the reviews were in, but for now I could relax and consider it a job done—hopefully well done.

Caroline had been a good sport all day, playing the four roles she was cast in. Changing back into my regular clothes, I met the crew outside, who were still bubbling from the day. I felt a hand take mine. It was a familiarity I loved as I turned and smiled at Caroline.

"Can we go back to the hotel? I'm a little tired." She looked at me with doe eyes.

I squeezed her hand. "Want to order room service?" I winked at her.

"I'll take room service if you're serving." She let out a little girlish giggle at her own joke, and I pulled her away from the group, headed toward the car.

"You know, you looked like versions of you in those scenes."

I looked at Caroline. "How so?"

"Well, you maintained control on all the scenes. Not the spotlight so much but the control factor was definitely there." She paused. "I guess you were wearing a more socially appropriate Mistress-hat." Her tone was endearing, but I couldn't tell if there was a slight annoyance behind her calm expression.

I thought about it for a second. "I guess I was. I'm sorry, it was unintentional."

She shrugged. "Doesn't bother me, but ever since we started doing the more dominatrix, erotic stuff, I've made more mental notes." She continued to look forward as we walked. "For example, you always get the door, you reach for the bill, you always insist on carrying the shopping bags, you pretty much always drive unless we have a driver. You even manage all the travel arrangements and documents." She smiled. "You even proposed."

"I guess." Still unsure if I was in trouble for the shoot, I retorted, "But you took the spotlight of being the love of my life in all of them."

"I think, and I'm guessing, that you subconsciously think of me as an equal but still want to dominate." She squeezed my hand. "I want you to dominate. I just thought it was an interesting observation."

I don't know how else to be.

The parking lot was empty and poorly lit. Traffic could be heard a few streets away, and the crew's voices were becoming more and more muffled as they walked away. Unlocking the car, I reached for the passenger door handle, stopping short of opening it. I pushed Caroline gently against the car, her ass pressed against me.

I want to bite this ass.

"Are you sure you want me to dominate, in any scene, in any situation?" I continued to whisper in her ear, "I could take you right here." I rested my hand on her hip, hugging her closer to me as I pushed against her. She tried to turn to face me, but I held her hand steady against the car window. I saw a smile flicker across her face, the corner of her eye locking with mine. I kissed her cheek, making my way to her ear, nibbling on her ear lobe gently. She let out a shudder. I slowly moved my hand from her hip, running my hand over the fabric of her jeans, running my fingers between her legs. She shuddered again.

"I want you," she muttered, eyes closed. "I want you to dominate me."

I kissed behind her ear, working my way down her neck. I let my fingers rub against her more purposefully. Her breathing heightened as I teased her. I wanted so badly to peel her clothes from her body as I fondled her.

"You know that drives me crazy," Caroline whispered.

"I know." I smiled a little, still kissing her bare shoulder. I kept my fingers firm against her, feeling her tension build. Caroline was fully enthralled in the moment, so I lingered a little longer, but not too long. I left her wanting more, hoping she was wet for me.

She protested a little. "Hey, that's not fair. You're such a tease."

"You love me for it though. Come, let's go back. I want to do bad things to you." I kissed her on the lips as I opened the car door.

She sighed deeply, looking at me with exasperation. "Yeah, yeah I love you too—control freak."

I rolled my eyes. "Just get in the car and let your controlling fiancée drive you to the hotel to dominate you properly." She met my eyes as I shut the door, blowing an air kiss as I crossed the front of the car. A quirky smile had formed on her face.

****

I closed the hotel door behind us. Leaving the lights dim, I started where we had left off, pushing her against the door. Caroline was anxious to get my clothes off as she started unbuttoning my shirt. I held her hands steady in mine and kissed her deeply, bringing her hands to her sides and pushing my hips into hers. I unzipped her jeans. She shoved them down her legs, letting them fall to the floor. I ran my fingers over her, feeling her wetness through the fabric of her thong.

"Someone's excited," I teased. "You can do better than that, though, can't you my little one?"

Caroline's eye glinted with excitement. "Yes, Mistress."

I pulled her satin tank top over her head, leaving her in her underwear. "Come." I led her to the bedroom to stand facing the window. The sprawl of the city was vast below us, without a building to obscure the view. I placed her hands on the windowpane, letting my lips caress her shoulder. "Wait, and don't move," I ordered her. I removed my shirt and jeans, down to my usual basic black, lace underwear set. I kept my heels on. The additional height made me tower over Caroline's petite frame. I fumbled quickly for my bag of toys and put them on the nightstand, ready for action.

Returning to Caroline, frozen in anticipation by the

window, I brushed myself against her, running my nails down her back gently. She squirmed a little—she was always a bit ticklish. "Stay still," I said in a barely audible tone. "And close your eyes."

The lights of the city kissed her face, accentuating her bone structure and the laugh lines she wore so well. Her eyelashes cast a shadow on her cheeks while her lips kept perfectly together. I took her hair clip out, letting her hair cascade around her shoulders. The warmth of the sun had brought out a slightly darker complexion of her otherwise pale skin.

She's so beautiful.

I stood behind her now, kissing her back, kneeling to bite her ass. I ran my hands down her soft legs, pulling her thong down simultaneously. I grazed my nails up her inner thighs, and she squirmed. I planted my fingers gently against her clit, awakening any last dormant nerve in her body. She struggled not to move her hands. Her breath quickened as her legs began to quiver. She bent over farther, and I cupped her, pulling her ass out. I let my fingers slide into her wet slit—two went in easily. Caroline exhaled, a little relieved. I slid a third inside of her and I could tell, as she spread her legs willingly, she wanted more.

I stood, teasing her clit, still with wet fingers. "Can you handle more, my little one?"

She nodded, letting a smile form on her supple lips. I led her to the bed, keeping her on all fours. I reached for a silicone anal plug and teased her pussy with it, getting it wet.

"Do you want this?"

"Yes, Mistress." Caroline's voice was steady.

I kissed her thighs and ass, encouraging her body

to relax. I stroked her back, careful not to tickle her, and pushed her cheeks apart. Pushing the toy gently in, I whispered, "Deep breath." As she exhaled, she accepted the bulk of the plug. I moved it ever so slightly against the rim of her and watched Caroline's face enjoy the sensations. I brought my fingers back to her clit, keeping one hand on the toy, rotating it continuously. I felt her dripping into my palm. I waited for the inevitable—her body shook a little as her fingers gripped the sheets, her back flexing as the rush of pleasure took hold of her. I kept my hands steady, increasing pressure ever so slightly as her climax ended, hoping I would encourage it to linger a little longer. Her head fell heavily before she looked back at me.

"Wow." She smiled. "I like that thing." She turned over, inviting me to lie beside her. I did so very willingly.

Looking into her eyes, I wanted nothing more than to hold her close and never let go. "I love you, Caroline. I always will."

She pushed a few loose strands of hair away from my face. "I love you too."

We stayed a moment there, lying comfortably in the moment. I watched as she scanned my face, seemingly looking for an answer. I raised my eyebrows in anticipation. She got shy and looked away again, smiling ever so slightly.

"Yes?" I asked. "Out with it. I'll drag it out of you eventually."

She turned to me and held my gaze. "So, I've been doing some research. You, when you're being Mistress, are really...nice. Too easy."

I laughed. "Research? How am I too easy?"

"You're never mean to me, and you never make me do things for you."

"Why would I be mean to you?"

"Isn't that what a Mistress is supposed to be?"

I shrugged. "I guess I have my own take on it. I like flirting with the control aspect, but I love you and respect you. I always want to protect you and would never want to cause you harm, even if it's out of fun or being asked for."

She looked almost a little disappointed. "Never mean?"

"I've used a whip before," I reminded her.

"You tapped me like I was a little kid getting a spanking." She smiled at me coyly.

"I don't want to hurt you," I retorted again. "Are you a participant in this to make me happy or because you like being subservient?"

"Both, I guess. I was intrigued to learn more. It's not something I've ever experienced before you and me. You know that." She paused again, collecting another ounce of courage. "So, what is the most...out-there thing you've done?"

A slight giggle escaped my lips.

Too cute.

I tried to keep composure. "I don't know if you'll like it, but there's these little electrolysis devices that add electrical stimulus to different parts of the body. You'll have a laughing fit probably, since you're so ticklish."

Her eyes were wide. "Doesn't that hurt?"

"Nah, it feels like a buzzing on the skin. I haven't done any of the extreme versions of that. I'm sure there are people who have hurt themselves by using equipment not meant for that purpose. People go too far sometimes."

"What else have you done?" Caroline's curiosity was abundant.

I lay back and stared at the ceiling, trying to think. "I've tried my fair share of toys and variations of them. There's things I can't get my head around still."

"Like?"

"Vaginal clamps?" I offered. "Those still scare me. Nipple clamps are bad enough, let alone ones down there."

She raised an eyebrow. "That sounds a little uncomfortable."

I nodded. "I have never wanted to try things with you, or with anyone I've been with, unless I knew the impact of them. Pain tolerance is individually set, but I'm sure as hell not going to subject someone else to a level of pain I can't handle. That doesn't seem fair."

"What size is the thing in my ass?" she asked, wiggling her perfect butt muscles.

"Beginner's size." I clarified. "Smallest they come."

"Would I like a bigger one?"

"Eager on the ass plugs, are we?" I laughed. "They're one of my favorite accessories too. Yes, you probably would like the bigger ones. They have a lot of kinds, even inflatable. I may just have one in the drawer back home." I winked at her.

"How come we've never gone to one of those shops together?" she asked, running a finger along the top of my breasts.

I turned toward her again. "Babe, we have, a long

time ago, and you were mute. Your face turned a million shades of red, and you basically ran out of there."

She looked through me, trying to recall. "I kind of remember, that was, what—five? Six years ago? I've changed since then. We were just friends back then and you know, since now I know what I've been missing, I should probably see what my options are." She had a girlish smile on her face, full of flirtation and mischief.

"I might know just the place." I returned her playful smile. "We will get you some other attire as well." I took her hand in mine. "My beautiful girl deserves to be adorned in beautiful things."

She let out a sheepish giggle. "You honestly need to wear something other than black underneath."

"I have other colors," I began in protest, only to be met with disapproving eyes. "Fine, fine, we can both get things." I pulled her over onto her stomach, kissing her shoulder. I slapped her ass lightly. "You should probably take that out. They're not the most comfortable long term."

She nodded, wiggling her butt cheeks in reply as she rolled off the bed. "You know what? I'm hungry," she pouted.

I smiled at the familiarity of the statement. "Oh, my dear Carol, you're always hungry after we play!"

"Can we do room service? I don't feel like leaving." She trotted to the bathroom, her strides awkward with the anal intrusion. "What do they have?"

I couldn't help but smile as I watched her move off. I opened the menu and scrolled through it. "Don't worry, I'll order for us." I called down for the food, hoping it would come quickly. Still in nothing but bra, panties, and heels, I waited for Caroline to come back out, swiping through my emails on my phone. "I brought wine with us. Would you like a glass?"

Caroline's eyes didn't leave mine. "You can't lie there like that and just ask me if I want wine while you're on your phone in underwear and heels. That's mean." She came up behind me and pushed open my legs, coming to kneel between them. She whispered softly, "Remember, you don't like being mean to me."

I started to turn over, but she pushed my ass down with firm, loving hands.

"You always get to be in control," she said softly. "Let me please you for once, at least let me try." I felt her lips graze my back, working their way down to the waistband of my thong. She slipped them off with gracious fingers. I found myself not knowing how to react—struggling with the conflict of wanting to please and the strong discomfort of letting go.

"Relax, baby," she whispered, feeling my angst. I closed my eyes as her soft caresses started to work their magic on my legs, her nails running down my back, then shifting to grip my ass cheeks. She slipped a hand under my waist, flipping me over. I rested my feet on the bed, my heels forcing my pelvis toward her. She eagerly started kissing my inner thighs, her kisses turning to licks as she took my clit in her mouth.

Breathe. Relax. Try to enjoy.

My body started to quiver as her tongue circled magically, making my back arch and my hands grip the sheets below. I tried to force my head to go blank, enjoy the moment and the rush of blood through my body.

I dared to look down, watching such a beautiful

girl, with hair pulled to one side and lips so pink with warmth, take the time to love me and try to pleasure me. Her sincere attempt made me love her all the more.

She nibbled a little bit on my clit, and my body twitched.

Breathe. Just let things happen.

I could feel my body failing me. I felt the sexual tension dissipate.

Fuck. I don't know how to stop this.

I looked at her, hoping she hadn't noticed yet.

I need to save the moment before it's gone. I can do this.

I calmed my panic a little and decided to take hold of my own clit, gently bringing Caroline up to meet my mouth instead. She put up the slightest bit of resistance but complied. Compromising, Caroline kept up with her fingers inside of me. I finally relaxed again and focused on the tender kisses Caroline was giving me. The way she tasted, how soft her skin was against mine, the way her hair smelled as it curtained my face. Finally, my body decided to let fate take hold. Sensations shot up my back, forcing it into a bold arch. My eyes rolled back, encouraging the flood of sensations down my spine as one hand took hold of the sheet and the other caressed her waist, bringing her slightly into me. As Caroline helped me finish, my breathing settled, and I was left with goosebumps on my arms.

She looked at me with brilliant eyes. "I knew I couldn't be that bad," she teased. "You still stopped me though." Her voice was quiet, a little disappointed.

"I told you I was tough." I fought not to show my own frustration.

She maintained her soft-spoken voice. "I will break

down those walls one day."

I smiled, agreeing with her. "One day." I pushed her hair out of her face. "Thank you." I kissed her, tasting a bit of myself on her lips.

Chapter Nineteen

I stood in front of the mirror, alone in the room, silently staring at myself. I could hear the voices chattering outside in the courtyard. Almost everyone that we invited had flown to the Amalfi Coast to join us—even my mother had decided it would better to get on the boat rather than be left behind.

It was a beautiful day for a wedding. The sun was shining still, the air warm from the day, the sea breeze gentle. The courtyard was neatly lined with white chairs overlooking the coastline. Flowers were in abundance—scattered in miniature and grand arrangements around the chairs and altar, with petals lining the runner. The ceremony would happen exactly twelve minutes past seven in the evening, just enough time to say our vows and have amazing sunset pictures. I peeked out the window. The sun was starting to descend. It was nearly seven, and I heard a knock at the door.

"Honey," my dad's voice softly questioned behind the door. "It's time."

I walked carefully over to open the door. "Hey."

He was a man of few words, but his mouth gaped open, barely letting out the words. "You look…you look so beautiful. Amazing."

I felt my cheeks flush. "Thanks, Dad." I took one last look in the mirror. The elegant silhouette of the dress formed carefully around my breasts and waist, flowing out delicately to meet the floor. The soft ivory fabric was embellished with gold and white crystals— not overpowering, but just enough to add some sparkle. Caroline had made the dress using a different model so that it would still be somewhat of a surprise as to what it would look like on me. She had done a fantastic job, per usual.

I had opted for no veil but left my hair to flow naturally, only adorning it with a simple crystal fastener on my picture-ready side. I held the bouquet of soft pink and ivory roses, mixed with local white flowers, the arrangement grand but simple all at the same time.

"Let's go," I said, taking my dad's extended arm.

We walked down the steps and hallway in silence, but a smile spread on my face as the music changed to welcome me into the ceremony space. My mother stood as we approached her, her expression kind. She had grown less angry about the relationship as the year since our announcement had passed by.

"I'm proud of you," she said. "You found someone you love, you defended it, and you've nurtured it. I'm truly happy for you."

"Thanks, Mum." I looked at her watering eyes and figured that even if she was lying, at least she was trying all the more to accept.

I kissed my parents on either cheek and took my position at the altar, handing my bouquet to my mother to hold. Both Caroline and I had decided that bridal parties were not a good fit for us since we were one another's best friends. Only family and immediate friends had been invited to join us. The whole wedding guest list had never teetered over sixty-five. I felt my heart beat faster as I waited in anticipation, fiddling with the substantial engagement ring on my right ring finger that Caroline had insisted I needed.

The music changed once again, and it was Caroline's turn to walk down the aisle. I barely noticed her brother, whom I had never met prior to this wedding trip, as he walked with Caroline slowly. The corners of my mouth lifted, and I felt my face beaming. She met my gaze and grinned widely, almost forgetting to acknowledge her mother who waited for her.

Caroline's dress was a very fitted lace gown that fell to the floor and had an ornate neckline of decorative crystals. The small train, also adorned with crystals, trailed behind her. It was perfect on her small frame. She kissed her mother and brother on either cheek. Giving her bouquet away, Caroline came to stand in front of me. She was almost the same height.

Recalling the many Saturdays we spent trolling through Paris, Milan, and New York, I couldn't help but laugh and quietly murmur, "So, this is why we spent half a lifetime looking for the tallest platforms any designer has ever made."

"Maybe," she said, puckering her lips ever so slightly. "And you know you love me for it."

"Of course." I shook my head. "You look phenomenal." I wanted to kiss her so badly but knew I had to wait another ten minutes.

We turned to face the pastor, an older gentleman, standing patiently, holding his ceremony notes.

"We are gathered here today..." His voice carried into the crowd. I looked at Caroline, standing before me, hands in one-another's, and I got ready to say my part. I hadn't written them down or even practiced but I knew that my tongue would find all the words. "…have written their own vows." The pastor paused and looked at me, prompting me to speak.

"Carol, we've been through hell and high water together. We've been there for one another through life's challenges, and we've continued to press one another and ourselves to be better. I couldn't ask for someone more supportive, more giving, or more caring. Every day I get to be with my best friend. Every day I get to share my time with someone I love. You are the epitome of what the love of my life and my partner in crime could be. With you by my side, and me by yours, we will conquer whatever we take on and, at the end of the day, still be mastering our relationship. I trust you, I respect you, and, most of all, I love you."

A single tear rolled down her cheek. I took her left hand and placed the diamond eternity band on her finger. I wiped away the tear as Caroline cleared her throat, taking out a little slip of paper from the top of her dress. Her voice was calm despite the visible shake of her hand.

"You accept me for who I am—all my faults and imperfections. You know me better than I know myself, and you always manage to make me smile, no matter what kind of day I've had. We are not perfect as individuals, but we are closer to perfect when we are together. I can't imagine my life without you by my side. I will always love you." Caroline looked up from her paper. "I will always love you," she repeated. "I promise." She placed the solid gold wedding band on my finger as the sun was half-settled on the horizon. I heard the click of the photographer's camera go off several times.

The pastor looked at each of us. "By the power invested in me, I hereby pronounce you partners in life, in love, and as wives."

Caroline was beaming as I placed one hand behind her head and the other on her waist, pulling her in. I didn't care about the lipstick as I planted a generous kiss on her lips. Her eyes fluttered to meet mine and we broke our lips away. She smiled broadly.

I get to look at that smile for the rest of my life.

The clapping of our friends and family was muffled by the enthralling moment. It was the loud shouts from Georgi and Federico that broke the spell. We walked back down the aisle, careful not to trip over one another. Allie showered us in rose petals as we walked by her, and she blew us a hearty air kiss.

****

The sun had long set, and the food had come and gone. Caroline was on the dance floor with her brother, being her silly self. My parents were on the floor too, along with the majority of both our families. I stared at Caroline's mother, Angela, who had brought a very handsome young man as her date. He was overly doting, and she loved the abundance of attention. As I stayed seated at the head table, I couldn't help but smile to myself.

Who knew? After everything, the girl I'd end up with was the one girl I had earmarked as a 'friend only.'

I felt a tap on my shoulder. I looked back at the girl dressed in a crisp white shirt, unbuttoned to show a modest amount of cleavage, navy pencil skirt, and mid-heeled shoes. Her dark, burgundy hair was pinned back in a half-up-half-down do. Her lips colored with a slight red-pink lipstick framed her white teeth perfectly.

"May I take your plate?" she asked sweetly.

I nodded. "Yes, thank you." I tried not to let my eyes linger on the girl's tight, well-rounded ass as she walked away. I refocused on my glass, watching the ruby red liquid kiss the sides. I sighed a little.

The familiar voice behind me took the words from my brain. "She was cute. Great ass."

I looked up to meet Caroline's eyes. "You noticed?"

She laughed. "Babe, I may be older, but my eyes are not blind! So, what did you think?"

"About the girl?" I waited for the eye roll and nod before continuing. "Yeah, she was cute." I continued to maintain my nonchalant demeanor.

Caroline took her seat beside me, taking a sip of her glass. She whispered, "Does Mistress want another pet?"

I raised my eyebrow, looking up at her from under the furrow of my brow. "Does my little one want a pet?"

She kissed my lips. "I've never had one so, I won't know till I try. And if you are willing, I'm willing." She paused, watching the girl as she cleaned up plates. "Dare I say, even wanting to try."

I smirked a little. "It could be arranged." I took her hand in mine as we continued to survey the crowd.

This is going to be fun.

Epilogue

We sat side-by-side on the bench seat, her hand on my knee, my arm resting on the back of the blue velvet couch, around her shoulders. I felt the warmth of her bare skin as I stroked her gently with my fingers. I sipped my Cabernet slowly, letting the robust liquid coat my mouth before swallowing.

The room was alive with a mix of patrons, all dressed in their personal touch of eroticism. The lights were low, and the drinks flowed effortlessly from the bar. Lining the walls were topless dancers, of both genders, wearing dark leather bottoms and PVC. They were masked for the most part. The air smelled sweetly of vanilla and a slight hint of musk.

There were other Dominatrix or Mistresses in the room, but mainly Masters or Misters, Playmates, submissives, and androgynous, full-face-masked persons. A scantily dressed male, with a puppy's tail, was being led by his master to join another couple at the other end of the bench seating. They accepted the approach, and exchanges were made before the master clinked his glass against theirs, making his sub sit and wait for instructions. The couple, dressed in anime and leathers, left with the master and his sub, to the private rooms down the hall. There was no judgement here. People were free to be who they were—whomever or

244

whatever they wanted to be that day. And, as long as the house rules were followed, anything was game.

Caroline had opted for a red teddy that held its structure around her bust. She had taken to making her own garments lately. Private label for her Mistress, she would tell me. The teddy had gold facets down the back and lace detailing around the small of her back, leading down to her ass. Pairing that with black platforms, I had struggled to not jump her before we left our apartment. It left little to the imagination, but the chain choker that adorned her neck, the light chain leash, and the matching masks we both wore, set the tone about our intentions perfectly. I had chosen a black body suit that hugged every curve and prominently displayed my cleavage. The black, lace-up, thigh-high boots were a little over-the-top, but Caroline had insisted they completed the outfit. I had grown to understand that Caroline really loved pushing her boundaries, and I enabled every moment of it.

"What about her?" Caroline asked as she tapped my knee, pointing with her jaw at the woman who was walking toward the bar.

I watched as the brunette took a seat on a stool and ordered herself a drink. No one followed her, no one came to join her. Her outfit, a charcoal gray and pink trim corset, Barbie-pink platforms and black tutu, which did not cover any of her ass, suggested that she would be submissive.

I can work with that.

I looked at Caroline, silently asking for certainty, and she nodded in response.

"All right, let's give her a go."

I always let Caroline pick the subs first. We had the

same taste in women, so it almost always worked out. Plus, I wanted to make sure she was on-board with whomever joined us.

Caroline assumed her position behind me as we walked over to the young woman still sitting alone at the bar. I stood off to the side, ushering Caroline forward to introduce herself. I didn't like talking to subs. I had no reason to talk to them, but the sub and Caroline needed to get along. Plus, as the Dominant, I never had to talk if I didn't want to. I motioned for the bartender to provide a round of drinks for the three of us after I got the nod from Caroline. The girl smiled at me. I returned it, but not overly so.

"What would you like me to call you?" I asked her.

"Brittany, Mistress," she responded, taking a sip of her drink.

"Do you like my lovely girl here?" I pulled Caroline's chain a little so she would come closer. She was obedient and stood behind my shoulder.

Brittany nodded. "Yes, Mistress, I do."

"Do you want to please her?"

She nodded again. "And you, if I may, Mistress." She kept her eyes low, indicating she had some prior experience being a sub.

I checked Caroline's expression once more. She was still pleased with her choice, so I continued, "Then, shall we retire to a more private space so you two can play together?"

Caroline extended her hand to lead Brittany. They walked stride in stride behind me as we walked casually down the hall to find an available room.

About the Author

A romantic lesbian fiction author with a flirtatious amount of kink.

~*~

Visit Aleksandra Amante at
http://aleksandraamante.com

Also Available
from The Wild Rose Press, Inc.
and major retailers.

Cuffed & Collared
Boston's Brave Book Three
By Samantha Cayto

Regan Malloy is a dedicated homicide detective married to her job. A tough woman who holds her own when it comes to the opposite sex, she is nevertheless resigned to lonely nights with fantasy men. When a serial killer targets wealthy submissive men from an upscale BDSM club, Regan is convinced the killer is a woman and goes undercover.

Kyle Ramsey is a topnotch litigator juggling life as a divorced father and a workaholic. Raised to be strong and to always take charge, he has trouble trusting that anyone else can get the job done. When he finds his good friend murdered, he mounts his own investigation despite Regan's warning not to interfere.

Regan is furious to find the sexy lawyer at the club but can't deny her attraction or her need to dominate him. Kyle discovers more than clues as, to keep from blowing their cover, the fiery cop demands obedience. Together, they embark on a journey to explore this new world of hidden desires, but the road could take a dangerous turn when they cross paths with the killer.

Also Available
from The Wild Rose Press, Inc.
and major retailers.

Neapolitan Nights
One Scoop or Two
By Paul Lonardo

I don't want to go home after the spring semester ends. I'm nineteen, away from home for the first time, and…I've met someone, a boy from my psychology class. I'm tempted to see where this flirtation leads, and when my professor offers me a summer job, I have the perfect excuse to stay. But Sam has a secret that I'm not sure I can accept, a secret that would initiate exploration of a whole new side of my sexuality. If I'm brave enough.

Thank you for purchasing
this publication of The Wild Rose Press, Inc.

For questions or more
information contact us at
info@thewildrosepress.com.

The Wild Rose Press, Inc.
www.thewildrosepress.com